PUBLISHER'S NOTE

This is the twelfth volume of Charlie Small's amazing journal. A fusty old businessman found the notebook in the luggage rack on a train. It was dog-eared and dirty but filled with the most amazing tales of derring-do. The man recognized Charlie's writing and as soon as he arrived at his station, he brought the journal straight to us. Here is the thrilling conclusion to Charlie Small's incredible adventures!

Does Charlie make it home? Will there be other journals to find? Only time will tell. So, keep your eyes peeled and if you do come across a curious-looking diary or see an eight-year-old boy carrying an explorer's kit, please let us know at the website:

www.charliesmall.co.uk

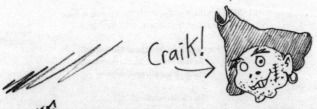

Craik!

THE AMAZING ADVENTURES OF CHARLIE SMALL (400)

Notebook 12

THE FINAL SHOWDOWN

Watch it, sonny!

Beware of yetis

CHARLIE SMALL JOURNAL 12: The Final Showdown
A DAVID FICKLING BOOK 978 1 849 92024 7

Published in Great Britain by David Fickling Books,
a division of Random House Children's Publishers UK
A Random House Group Company

This edition published 2011

3 5 7 9 10 8 6 4

The Random House Group Limited supports The Forest Stewardship
Council (FSC®), the leading international forest certification organisation.
Our books carrying the FSC label are printed on FSC® certified paper.
FSC is the only forest certification scheme endorsed by the leading
environmental organisations, including Greenpeace. Our
paper procurement policy can be found at
www.randomhouse.co.uk/environment

MIX
Paper from
responsible sources
FSC® C016897

Set in 15/17 Garamond MT

DAVID FICKLING BOOKS
31 Beaumont Street, Oxford, OX1 2NP

www.**randomhousechildrens**.co.uk
www.**totallyrandombooks**.co.uk
www.**randomhouse**.co.uk

Addresses for companies within The Random House Group Limited can be found at:
www.randomhouse.co.uk/offices.htm

THE RANDOM HOUSE GROUP Limited Reg. No. 954009

A CIP catalogue record for this book is available from the British Library.

Printed and bound in Great Britain by Clays Ltd, St Ives PLC

NAME: Charlie Small

ADDRESS: Fortune City

AGE: I'm an eight-year-old boy who's lived for four hundred years!

MOBILE: 07713 123█

SCHOOL: St Beckham's

THINGS I LIKE: The Air-rider; Snipe and the Outcasts; Mum and Dad; Jumbo

THINGS I HATE: Joseph Craik (my arch-enemy); Bush Spiders; lonely Yeti

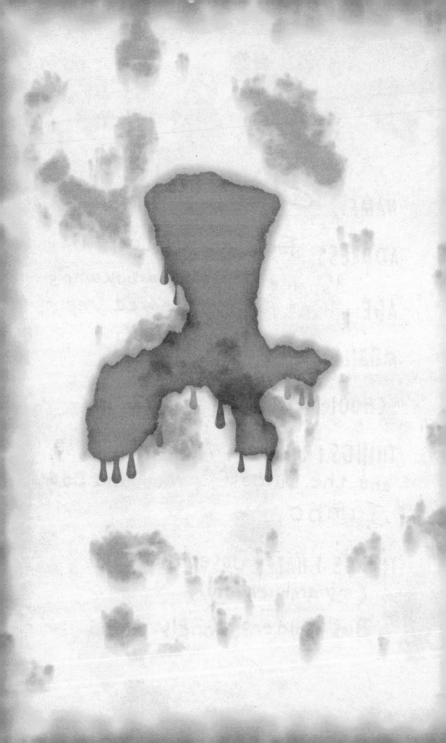

If you find this book, PLEASE look after it. This is the final account of my remarkable adventures.

My name is Charlie Small and I am four hundred years old, maybe even more. But in all those long years, I have never grown up. ~~Some~~ Something happened when I was eight years old, something I can't begin to understand. I went on a Journey... and I'm still trying to find my way home. Now, although I've come face to face with an enormous and hairy yeti, been attacked by huge, wind-blown spiders and nearly arrested by a race of strange rat-like people, I still look like any eight-year-old boy you might pass in the street.

I've climbed mountains, crossed a vast, muddy desert and been chased by a dangerous villain through the carriages of a high-speed train. You may think this sounds fantastic, you could think it's a lie, but you would be wrong. Because EVERYTHING IN THIS BOOK IS TRUE. Believe this single fact and you can share the most incredible Journey ever experienced.

Charlie Small

The mountains of
the Jagged Edge

On The Mountains Of The Jagged Edge

I cowered behind a large slab of rock, holding my breath and straining my ears. I could definitely hear something; a scuffing, padding sound that was almost lost in the noise of the wind that blew across the top of the mountain. What could it be?

From the moment I set out on my journey, I was sure someone was on my trail. Every now and then I stopped and looked behind me, studying the landscape through my telescope. I didn't see anything other than shifting shadows, but I was certain someone was there, watching my every move.

I'd been zooming along on the Air-rider, an incredible hovering scooter invented by my friend

The incredible Air-rider: it goes like a rocket!

Jakeman, but when I reached the Jagged Mountains, I had to stop. The rock-strewn cliffs were too steep for the scooter, so I had to haul it up behind me with my home-made lasso. Finally, after hours of exhausting climbing, I scrambled onto the windy top of one of the peaks and dragged the Air-rider after me. I looked around the lonely mountaintop. It seemed deserted, but then I heard the scuffing, padding noise . . .

The swirling wind made it impossible to tell where the noise was coming from, but it sounded close. I didn't want to hang around in the open, so I ran for one of the great spears of rock that jutted from the peak. I crouched down behind it, hoping the noise was just my crazy imagination playing tricks.

It wasn't! Now I can hear the padding of footsteps quite clearly, and the hoarse panting of breath as my pursuer shuffles around the mountaintop. It is snuffling and sniffing the air like some huge bloodhound. Help! I've just peeped round the edge of my hiding place and seen an enormous, white hairy foot on the other side of the rock. *Yikes!*

It was a yeti!

Yeti! ōō

Oh, brilliant! You'll never guess where I am now. I've been captured and I'm languishing in a dingy den. I don't know how I'll ever escape.

This is what happened.

I scrambled to my feet and darted away, desperately searching for an escape route, but the big-footed monster was right behind me. I turned to face him, and the blood froze in my veins. It was a yeti – an abominable, hairy-faced yeti!

The creature towered above me. He was three metres tall and covered in shaggy white hair. Two lime-green eyes shone out from a dark blue, leathery face and large, curved horns above a low brow gave him a brooding, menacing expression.

'Wah!' the yeti barked, showing a line of terrible teeth, and he stepped towards me. I took a pace back.

'Wah!' he repeated, lifting a massive hand and gesticulating to the far side of the mountaintop. The yeti's arms were even longer and thicker than Thrak's, the old silverback gorilla who had kidnapped me at the very start of my adventures.

He stepped forward again, and I retreated

again, but I was now backed against another of the soaring rock spears. The yeti gave a low growl and lifted his enormous hand towards me. It was big enough to crush my skull like a tangerine, and my knees started to wobble.

'Wah!' the beast barked again. I felt faint with terror, and my legs folded beneath me. As I fell, I was aware of being lifted high into the air. Then I blacked out completely.

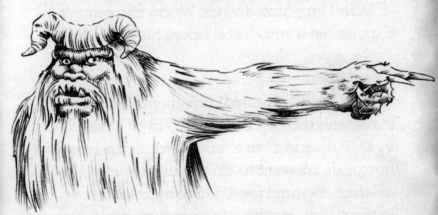

The Gruesome Den

When I came to, I was amazed to find that my head was still attached to my body – I'd feared the great hairy gonk was going to rip it off! It was dark and I wondered if it was already night-time, but when I propped myself up on my elbows and cautiously looked round, I saw I was lying on a thick pile of moss in a large, dim cave.

The dull red embers of a fire glowed in the centre of the floor; thin tendrils of acrid smoke climbed to the ceiling and filled the top half of the cave with dense smog. On the other side of the fire sat the yeti, watching me intently with his glowering, lime-green eyes.

'Wah!' he grunted when he saw me move, and slapped his stomach and licked his leathery lips.

Oh, cripes! I thought. *Now the thing wants to eat me!*

'Wah, wah,' repeated the yeti, pointing first at me, and then up into the cloud of smoke. I gazed up and gave a sigh of relief; the hairy horror didn't want to eat me all – he was offering *me* some food! Hanging from a hook in the ceiling amongst the swirling smoke was a huge side of meat. It was as big as a buffalo, with great curving ribs and knobbly white bones protruding from the dark, cooked flesh. Gruesome or what!

'Er, yes please,' I said, licking my lips and nodding. I didn't like the look of the grisly carcass, but I suddenly felt ravenous. I had

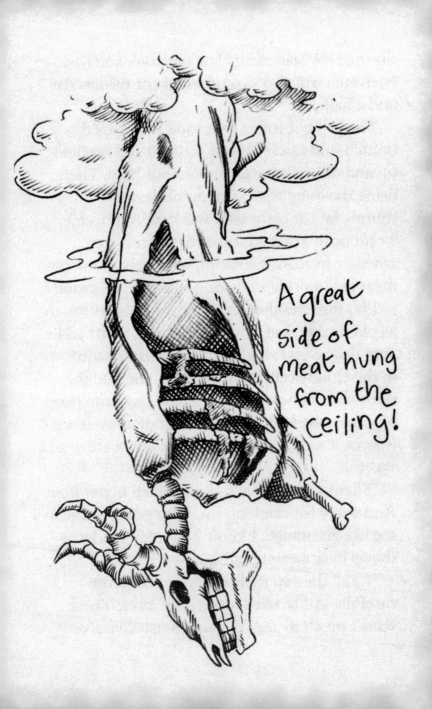

A great side of meat hung from the ceiling!

finished my last energy bar ages ago, and had been surviving on sips of water for the last day and a half.

The yeti got to his feet, took a V-shaped branch that stood against the wall and reached up and unhooked the humungous ham. Then, using the long, sharp nail on his leathery thumb, he cut off a slice and handed it to me. I cautiously reached forward, still not sure whether to trust this weird, wild beast, took the meat and quickly sat back on my pile of moss.

I bit into the slice, expecting it to be as tough as old leather, but it was tender and moist and very delicious! It had been smoked to a turn in the cloudy ceiling of the cave, and had the same spicy, smoky flavour as my favourite pizza topping. I had no idea what sort of meat it was (maybe a mountain troll) but I ate and ate until I was full.

'Thanks, Yeti,' I said. 'I feel much better now. And sorry for thinking you were going to crush me like an orange. I know I shouldn't judge things by appearances!'

'Wah!' the yeti replied, and watched me carefully as I strolled around the cave. There wasn't much to see. Yetis obviously live a very spartan life. Apart from a couple of piles of straw and moss, there were no creature comforts at all. The fire gave out just enough heat to warm the air around it, the smoky atmosphere made it difficult to breathe properly, and the whole cave smelled of damp fur. I needed some fresh air!

What a pong!

My Way Is Barred!

I looked around for the way out and saw a tunnel leading from the cavern. As I walked towards it, coughing and spluttering from a swirl of oily smoke that billowed down from above, the yeti immediately clambered to his feet and followed me.

I saw the bright light of the cave mouth at the far end of the passage, and realized it was still daylight outside, so I hadn't been unconscious for long. Good! I really wanted to get off the mountain before nightfall.

'Wah-wah-wah!' grunted the yeti, urgently.

'What's wrong?' I asked. 'I only want a bit of fresh air. It's so sme . . . um, stuffy back there.' By now I had reached the opening and saw a track leading up to the mountaintop one way, and down the mountainside the other.

Oh good, I thought. *That path is wide enough for me to ride my scooter!* But as I went to step outside, the yeti threw his arm across the opening and barred my way.

'WAH!' he bellowed. 'Wah, wa-wah.'

'Hold on, you great hairy oaf,' I cried, starting to panic all over again as he placed his massive hands on my shoulders and pushed me back into the cave. 'What do you think you're doing?' Had he changed his mind? Was I going to be suspended from a ceiling hook to gently smoke into a pink and tender ham?

'WAH!' ordered the yeti and pointed back at my bed of moss. 'WAH!'

I stumbled to the mossy mattress on wobbly

legs and flopped down, and as soon as I did, the yeti let out a satisfied sigh and sat down by the fire again. Now I got it! The yeti was lonely and didn't want me to leave – or wasn't going to let me leave, more like. Oh, flip. Now I was in a jam!

'Look, I'd like to stay,' I said in as calm a voice as I could manage, 'but I've got to get home in time for tea.'

'Wah,' replied the yeti. He didn't have much of a vocabulary. I cautiously stood up, and the yeti started to growl ominously.

'Look, I need to go to the loo,' I said, hoping he would let me out of his sight long enough for me to make a run for it.

'Wah?' asked the yeti.

'The loo. You know, the toilet,' I said and started to hop about as if I were desperate, but the yeti thought it was a game and gave a bellow of a laugh. It was no good, so I sat down again but then realized I'd made a big mistake.

I hopped about as if I needed the loo!

'Loo!' he cried, delighted with this new word. Staring at me with a surly frown, he brought his fist crashing down, making the ground shudder and shake. 'Loo!' he yelled, and it dawned on me that the great oaf was demanding to see my antics again.

I got up and started to hop about and the yeti laughed until tears ran down his leathery cheeks into his coarse white coat. And every time I stopped the big buffoon would yell 'LOO!' at the top of his voice until I started leaping about again.

I tried to dance my way towards the tunnel and make a getaway, but as soon as he saw what I was up to, the yeti was on his feet and growling an unmistakable warning. Oh, flip! What was I going to do?

A Close Run Thing

The yeti kept me dancing for hours. Every time I stopped he cried out, and if I refused to wriggle and squirm he roared, stamping around the cave in a terrible temper like a ten-tonne toddler. It was terrifying, and after hours of wiggling and wriggling, I was ready to drop. I also *really* needed to go to the loo!

Then, late in the afternoon, the yeti gave a loud growl and held up his hand as a signal for me to stop dancing. He cocked his head on one side as if he were listening for something, and sniffed the air with his flat, blue nose. I listened too, but couldn't hear a thing above the rasping sound of the yeti's breathing.

With a satisfied grunt the yeti got to his feet and marched towards the cave mouth. Before he disappeared into the tunnel, he turned and pointed at me and then at the ground. 'Wah!' he snapped and then, thrusting his face towards mine, gave the most terrifying, nerve-jangling roar I've ever heard. 'WAAAHH!' It was like standing in a wind tunnel, and the hair was blown back from my forehead in the rush of musty wind from his gaping jaws.

'OK, OK, don't get your undies in a twist,' I said. 'I understand. I'm to stay here. Don't worry, I won't go anywhere.'

'Wah!' said the yeti, seeming satisfied. He patted me on the head with his massive paw, and then tried to crease his ugly mug into a friendly grin. He gave a wave goodbye and disappeared along the tunnel. What a loony!

As soon as he'd gone, I flopped down into the pile of moss, exhausted from my dancing and shaken by the power of the yeti's roar. I waited to get my breath back and then waited some more for my courage to return. When my legs had stopped shaking and I felt able to stand, I got to my feet, grabbed my rucksack and darted for the tunnel. I wouldn't get a better chance to escape than this.

I'd only got halfway along the tunnel, though, when I heard the monster coming back. Oh, bloomin' heck! I'd left it too long. I raced back to the cave and dived onto my mossy bed, just as the hairy horror reappeared. He had the limp carcass of a mountain goat over his shoulder. 'Wah,' he grunted, pointing at the poor beast, and licked his fat leathery lips.

'That was quick,' I said, as the yeti tied the

goat with a rope and hung it up in the smoke to cook. 'Too bloomin' quick, if you ask me,' I added under my breath. Then my new best friend sat down again, clapped his hands and barked at me. 'Wah!' he ordered. 'Loo!'

Oh flip, here we go again!

Flight To Freedom!

The yeti wasn't the brightest button in the box and was very easily amused. I danced and wriggled and wriggled and danced, but eventually he became quieter and finally drifted into a fitful sleep.

I waited until the hairy beast began to snore rhythmically and then very carefully crept inch by inch on all fours towards the exit. Once I had to freeze, waiting with bated breath as the yeti's snoring stopped with a series of stuttering grunts. I was sure he'd woken up and that I'd be caught trying to escape, but after an excruciating minute he started snoring again, and I continued to edge forward.

It was already getting dark when at last I reached the cave mouth. With a sigh of relief I got to my feet and dashed up the track to the mountaintop, where I'd left my precious Air-rider. I stepped onto the scooter's footplate, turned on the headlight and started the fans. The hover-scooter lifted from the ground and I drove it carefully over the rocky summit to the top of the track. Then, opening the throttle, I shot forward and threw up a cloud of dust in my wake as I careered back down the path. I was going to make it!

Or was I? As I veered round a bend, I got the shock of my life. The yeti was waiting for me outside his cave, fully awake and very, *very* annoyed.

'WAAAAAAH!' he bellowed and lifted up a large rock from the side of the path. For an instant I throttled down, slowing the scooter whilst I tried to think. The yeti hurled the rock straight at me and I swerved out of its path, doing a fancy sideways bunny-hop manoeuvre, as the boulder smashed on the ground beside me. Then, as the yeti stooped to pick up another missile, I saw an opening and drove the scooter forward.

'WAH!' yelled the creature. The coarse hair from one of his legs whipped my face as I shot past him, inches from the edge of the track, and sent a shower of stones tumbling over the sheer mountainside.

'Yeehah!' I cried, adrenalin pumping through my veins. Another boulder crashed to the

Waaaah! ground in front of me and
again I swerved out of its way.

'Waaaah! Waaaah!' The pitiful
call of the yeti suddenly sounded as
lonely and mournful as the horn of a ship
lost at sea. It made me feel quite mean, but I
wasn't going back! I crouched down to reduce
my wind resistance and pelted along the dark
track, swerving left and right as it skirted the
mountainside.

A Fitful Sleep zzzzz

And now it's morning, and the day has dawned
grey and chilly. I hardly got a wink of sleep
last night and I'm tired and aching all over. My
fingers are so stiff with the cold that I'm finding
it hard to hold my pencil.

I spent the night amongst the foothills of the
Jagged Mountains. Even when I'd reached the
base of the yeti's mountain I continued driving
as fast as I could, worried that he would follow
me down.

I steered through the growing dark along
a wide pass that snaked its way through the

mountain range. The silhouettes of towering peaks surrounded me on every side, and the headlight on my Air-rider picked out the looming shapes of contorted rocks, looking like gangs of grisly ghosts turned to stone.

As the pass narrowed, the night seemed to grow even darker. It became harder to see where I was going, and I decided I had to stop for the night. I found a deep, black recess in the side of a hill, curled up on the ground and pulled my tattered coat from my rucksack to use as a blanket.

I dozed restlessly, my eyes springing open

at the sound of every nocturnal animal that shuffled and scratched in the darkness. Blimey, it was like trying to sleep in the middle of a zoo!

The night seemed to last forever, but eventually a weak light dawned and I got up, stamping my feet on the ground to warm them. I rolled up my coat but, before stuffing it back in my rucksack, I checked through my explorer's kit. I emptied everything on the ground and this is what my kit now contains:

1) My multi-tooled penknife
2) A brand new ball of string (extra strong)
3) A water bottle
4) A telescope
5) A scarf (complete with bullet holes!)
6) A strange railway ticket (this has been in my rucksack all the time – where on earth did it come from?)
7) My journal
8) A pack of Wild Animal Collector's Cards (full of amazing animal facts)
9) A glue pen for sticking things in my notebook
10) A glass eye from the brave, steam-powered rhinoceros

11) The compass and torch I found on the sun-bleached skeleton of a lost explorer

12) The tooth of a monstrous megashark (makes a handy saw)

13) A magnifying glass (for starting fires, etc.)

14) A radio

15) My mobile phone with wind-up charger (to speak to Mum)

16) The (broken) skull of a Barbarous Bat

17) A bundle of maps and diagrams collected on my adventures

18) A bag of marbles

19) One smoke bomb, shaped like a metal ball

The shiny
metal smoke bomb

20) The broken, bony finger of an animated skeleton (handy for picking locks)
21) A length of vine that I use as a lasso
22) The spider-thread wristband that Jakeman gave me. I'm still wearing it but the mechanism has jammed and it can no longer shoot out its small, metal anchor on a long string. It's a real shame, because it was *brilliant* for climbing and swinging around like Spiderman!

I've just tried to ring Mum, to let her know I'm on my way home. I have charged up my mobile with its little wind-up charger, but I can't get a signal here amongst the mountains.

My journal is bang up to date now, and I'm ready to set off. I've turned on the GPS gizmo on the scooter's handlebars and tried to pinpoint my position on the map that Philly gave me. It's the most precious document I've ever owned, because it shows me where I can cross back into my own world. Here it is, so you can see just how far I've got to go (I'm *somewhere* amongst the foothills of the Jagged Mountains!).

I'll write more later.

The Great Waste

By mid-morning I had left the Jagged Mountains far behind, and was racing my scooter at top speed across the vast, flat and empty landscape called the Great Waste. It was a scorching hot day and the dry, cracked earth was littered with the sun-bleached skeletons of unfortunate animals that hadn't made it across the desert.

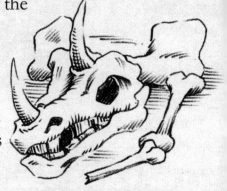

   An ugly-looking vulture circling overhead landed in the branches of a dead tree and peered down at me hungrily as I sped past. I shuddered, hoping that I wouldn't end up on his lunch time menu, and rocked back and forth on the Air-rider, urging it to go even faster.

I drove for hour after hour and by late afternoon I was sunburned, thirsty and very hungry.

A vile vulture!

I pulled up, got the water bottle from my rucksack and took a swig. Darn it! I tipped it up; the last few drops plopped onto the ground and soaked into the parched earth. Things were getting serious. I was alone in the middle of nowhere with no water and no food.

Suddenly a hot, strong wind started to blow. It came from the north and sent great sheets of dust swirling around my ankles. In the heat-shimmering distance I saw five dark spheres rolling over the ground towards me. They looked like the fat tumbleweed bushes I'd seen being blown across the ranges of the Wild West. *Maybe those bushes have got edible leaves,* I thought. *It's got to be worth a look.*

An Ill Wind

The tumbling bushes rolled towards me very quickly, but as they got closer they began to slow down even though the wind was still blowing hard.

That's weird, I thought. Then the bushes came to a stop and I stared at them in absolute horror. Each olive-green bush was about half a metre tall and had a row of four eyes, as dark and shiny as blackcurrant pastilles, peering from beneath a crown of leafy, waving branches! Only they *weren't* branches, and they *weren't* covered with fluttering, edible leaves. They were wriggling legs covered in long strands of greasy, green hair. I was staring at a ghastly species of spider, with a hundred hairy legs sprouting from all over their bodies. *Ugh!* I hate spiders!

The wriggling creatures had hitched a lift on the strong wind, but now they tiptoed about nervously on a forest of legs. They had two horny fangs and a revolting, dribbling crimson mouth that opened and closed sideways like the doors to a cupboard. My stomach heaved at the sight of them.

A bush spider
Ugh!

All Tied Up!

The wind died down as quickly as it had started and everything became eerily silent. Too late, I realized the shuffling spiders had surrounded me and were edging forward, hissing like bad-tempered snakes. I was still wearing the cutlass I'd found on the skeleton of the bloodthirsty pirate, Sabre Sue, and I drew it from its shiny scabbard.

'Get back!' I yelled, stepping from the Air-rider and swishing the gleaming blade back and forth. 'Get back or I'll slice you to pieces, you cretinous creepy-crawlies.' I swished the blade in a wide circle a few centimetres from the ground, and the spiders in front of me hopped and skipped to avoid having their toenails trimmed – but then another spider attacked from behind.

It grabbed the leg of my jeans with its bony fangs, and tugged so hard I was thrown to the ground with a thump that knocked the wind right out of me. The spider snatched the cutlass from my grasp and snapped it between its fangs as if it were no tougher than a twig. Then it spat a stream of thick drool onto the blade; the sword began to fizz and bubble as it melted into a silvery liquid. *Oh yikes!* These things were even more dangerous than they looked!

I tried to get to my feet, but another of the bushy spiders leaped on my back, pinning me to the floor. Now all the spiders attacked. *Snip, snap!* They pecked at my sweatshirt with their bony mandibles, and shot out thin strings of tough, fibrous thread from their rear ends. The thread wound around my legs, binding them tightly together. 'Get off, you cretins!' I cried.

Then the salivating spiders dragged the rucksack from my back and its contents spilled onto the dusty ground.

Got you, you devils, I thought, because they had just made a BIG mistake. I lunged for the last of the metal smoke bombs Jakeman had given me, and just managed to grab it before it rolled out of reach. I smashed it on the ground and the eight segments of the sphere cracked open. A plume of pungent smoke poured into the air and a thick, choking cloud enveloped us.

As my eyes began to sting and I started to cough, I tied my scarf around my mouth for protection. The spiders hissed in distress and staggered around in the fog, trying to find a way out of the ever-expanding cloud.

'*Wee, wee, wee!*' Their bubbling squeals sounded like petrified piglets.

I felt along the ground for the megashark's tooth, grabbed it and hacked at the web around my legs. The threads snapped like wire as I sawed at them with the tooth's sharp edge; then

I was on my feet, stuffing everything I could find back into the rucksack. I stepped onto my scooter, gunned the engine and shot forward, barging two of the choking spiders out of my way.

As I raced across the desert, the wind started up again and a strong gust caught the dense, yellow cloud. It swirled the smoke round and carried it up into the air. I braked hard, turned the scooter and looked back, ready to scarper if the spiders were still on the attack – but they were no longer there. The muddy desert was empty! All that remained of the crawling creeps were five small, bubbling puddles in the mud. The sulphurous clouds must have dissolved them!

Feeling shocked and shaky, I revved the scooter's throttle and carried on with my journey, zooming past scatterings of ancient, fossilized animals and bony skeletons. After a

A fearsome fossilised fish!

while I began to relax, and when I spotted a lone, barrel-shaped cactus I slowed down and steered my scooter towards it.

Wary at first, in case it turned out to be another species of revolting insect, I tapped the cactus with my finger. Then, happy it *was* just a cactus, I lopped off the top with the megashark tooth, cut out a segment of white, juicy flesh and chewed it to a pulp, letting its cool, sweet juices trickle down my parched throat. It was delicious!

A slice of Juicy cactus!

Phoning Home

The night has descended quickly. One minute the sun was a shimmering ball low in the sky, and the next it dipped below the horizon and the world became pitch black. There are no stars in the sky, and no moon to help light my way; it soon became impossible to see where I was going, even with my scooter's headlight on, and I decided to make camp.

I am squatting on the ground, leaning against my rucksack and writing up my journal by the pale yellow beam of my torch. A chilly wind is

It was very dark and spooky!

blowing, but I'm quite cosy behind the shelter of my coat, which is hung between two sticks in the ground to act as a windbreak.

I've just phoned home.

'Charlie, is that you? Is everything all right?' asked Mum when she picked up the phone.

'Well, apart from being taken hostage by a very lonely yeti and attacked by some gross, gurgling, snipping, snapping bush spiders, everything's fine,' I replied.

'Sounds wonderful, dear,' said Mum.

'I'm sitting in the middle of a vast desert with no food and no water,' I continued.

'Ooh, that's nice,' said Mum cheerily. 'Wait a minute, Charlie. Here's your dad just come in. Now remember, don't be late for tea and don't forget to pick up a carton of milk on your way home.'

'Sure, Mum. See you soon,' I said and hung

up. She is stuck in a time loop and I'm used to her saying the same thing every time I call. Poor Mum, if she knew salivating spiders really had attacked her son, she'd go bananas!

Thinking about the spiders sent a shiver of disgust rippling down my spine, and I wondered if my Wild Animal Collector's Cards had anything to say about them.

PREDATOR
12

Bristling Bush Spiders

These revolting arachnids have a hundred hairy legs. They live in deserts and can quickly travel great distances by letting strong winds blow them across the plains—so watch out! Bush spiders can digest almost anything, as their saliva is a powerful acid. They disable their victims by wrapping them up in a strong cocoon of thread.

WILD ANIMAL COLLECTORS CARDS

I gave another shudder of disgust and quickly put the cards away. I had been very lucky to escape; another few seconds and I would have been fizzing and melting into a little pool of goo like my pirate's cutlass!

All of a sudden, the sun began to rise. It's five o'clock in the morning already, and I've been thinking and writing all night long! I don't feel tired, though – just very hungry. The air is clear, the sky is cloudless and I can see something flashing and sparkling on the distant horizon. It must be Fortune City! It's marked on my map and is directly on the route back to my world. Brilliant! I might be able to get something to eat there.

I'll write more later.

An Instant Ocean!

I belted towards the tiny glimmering shape on the horizon, but an hour later, it didn't seem to be any closer. Then, just as I thought it must be a mirage, the city suddenly appeared to grow and grow, and I began to see skyscrapers of every shape and size built on a tall mound of rock, like an island in the middle of the flat wasteland.

'*Yeehah!*  Only a few more miles to go,' I cried. 'Fortune City here I come.' But just as I said this there was a loud gurgling from beneath my feet and the ground started to rumble and shake as water seeped up from the tiny cracks in the dry mud. The flat desert began to fill up like a huge bath and soon the whole area was covered with a glistening sheet of water. Luckily, my scooter was just as happy hovering on water as on land; I drove it on, its fans humming like a hairdrier.

The water grew deeper and deeper, and I steered towards the safety of the city, which had now become an island in a vast sea. It was only a few hundred metres away and I could see a high, whitewashed wall snaking around the edge of the island.

Fortune City

Then another surge of water boiled up from below and a great wave rolled across the surface towards me. I tried to ride it like a surfer, but my wonderful Air-rider was whipped from under me and carried away by the powerful current. I splashed into the sea and rolled over and over in the boiling surf as I tried to find my feet, but by now the sea was much too deep for me to stand up.

I floundered around trying to get my bearings and then struck out for the island. I swam for all I was worth, but the weight of my rucksack quickly made my arms tire and my crawl soon became a weak doggy-paddle. I began gulping mouthfuls of water as I tried to stay afloat, and I didn't think I was going to make it. I decided to jettison my explorer's kit.

With my arms feeling like wet string, I slipped the rucksack from my back and was just about to let it sink to the bottom of the sea when a strong ocean swell lifted me up and swept me towards

My arms got so tired, they felt like wet bits of string!

the island. I was carried like a bobbing cork amongst the rocks that lined the shore and, grabbing hold of a barnacled boulder, I dragged myself from the swirling foam.

Despite feeling battered and bruised, I filled my empty water bottle from a rockpool before collapsing on the shore in exhaustion. I couldn't move for a long time.

Fortune City

The hot sun dried my wet clothes quickly and, as I got my breath back, I became aware of muffled noises from the other side of the high city wall. I could hear voices, the shuffling of hundreds of feet and the clanging of distant machinery.

Rising unsteadily, I scrambled over the sharp rocks to the base of the wall. It was much too high to climb, so I began walking, following the wall as it snaked around the island. It was tough-going. I had to climb over jagged boulders and jump over choppy inlets, but as it swept around the end of the island I saw two tall gates standing open in the wall. I staggered towards them, suddenly feeling weak with hunger after my treacherous and exhausting journey.

There was a roadway leading from a small quay built amongst the rocks up to the open gates. I climbed down onto its cobbled surface and followed it under a tall arch, and into Fortune City. Just inside the gates a street crossed at right angles, and it was thronged with people.

'Make way! Move aside there,' said an impatient, wheedling voice and a man tried to barge me out of the way. 'I'm in a hurry.'

'Pardon me,' I said huffily, and moved to one side as the man pushed past.

He was not much taller than me, and had a dumpy, round body with thin little legs and arms. His face looked stretched and elongated, as if someone had got hold of his nose and pulled as hard as they could. His hair grew almost down to his eyebrows, and with his large,

The people had a ratty look!

protruding teeth and small, black eyes he looked rather like a startled rat!

As I watched the moving mass of people, I saw that they *all* looked like scurrying, sharp-nosed rodents. Some were carrying briefcases, or talking on mobile phones. Others pushed heavily-laden handcarts and some, wearing long grey overcoats, were weaving through the crowd on strange one-wheeled mopeds.

On the opposite side of the swarming street stood a row of old buildings, and behind them sprouted a forest of glittering, glass skyscrapers. These were built so closely together they looked like rows of gleaming organ pipes, and the windows of each glass tower were only inches away from the windows of another.

I stepped into the noisy crowd and tried to cross to where the main street carried on through the centre of the town. After my days of lonely travel, the bustling crowd made my head start to spin. I became dizzy and confused, and the swarm of shuffling people carried me along with them.

"Scuse me,' I said as I was barged and buffeted from one person to another. 'Ouch, excuse me, oof! Do you know where I can get something to eat?' No one answered. They hurried along with blank staring eyes and determined, hungry expressions.

'Please, let me through,' I cried. Suddenly, I was sent spinning from the throng into another stream of rat-faced people swarming down the main street. I was swept along under the arches of a tall viaduct; a train, packed with people, rumbled over it.

High up on a stone tower, a big clock began to chime. I looked up and saw that it was nine o'clock in the morning. Like clockwork, the moving mass of people began to subside as they all streamed into the jungle of buildings. A minute later I was standing, dazed and confused, in a completely deserted street.

Skyscrapers crowded around the old buildings

It was a strange, higgledy-piggledy mixture of ancient and futuristic-looking buildings. There were old, three- and four-storey structures made of mellow, yellow stone and topped with orange-tiled roofs, and the shining spires of skyscrapers were packed into every available space. Just then a soft hum filled the air, as lights and computers and printers and copiers inside the buildings were turned on. A minute later, messengers began to appear, scuttling from one building to another with bundles of paper under their arms.

'Excuse me,' I asked as one man hurried past. He slowed down a fraction, looking at me curiously.

'Can't stop. Too much to do, too much to do,' he said in a hurried, piping voice and carried on.

'Excu . . . ' I began as another messenger sprinted by.

He didn't even bother to look at me, just called over his shoulder. 'Can't you see I'm busy?'

Right, I thought. *I've had enough of this.* And as yet another messenger rushed by, I reached out and grabbed him by the sleeve. 'Stop!' I begged.

'What do you think you're doing?' cried the messenger, his long, pointed nose twitching and his small, round eyes staring in alarm. 'You'll bring Fortune City to a standstill.'

'But I only want to know —' I began again, but the little man was stamping his feet impatiently and looking at a big brass pocket watch.

'I know I'm only a small cog,' he interrupted, pulling his sleeve from my grasp. 'But if you stop just one tiny cog, the wheels of industry will grind to a halt. Then where will we be, eh? Don't they teach you anything at school?' With that the man tutted and rushed away.

'Where can I get something to eat?' I called after him.

'In a restaurant!' he called over his shoulder.

Thanks a bunch, I thought as the man disappeared through the glass doors of a skyscraper. *Very funny, I'm sure.*

Swept Aside

I couldn't see any food stores along the wide avenue, so I decided to try a narrow side alley instead. It turned this way and that, with other passages leading off in all directions, and I was soon feeling lost. The passages were dim and creepy, with large posters pasted on the walls bearing slogans in bold, black type:

The alley led into a small, enclosed courtyard and here at last was a little group of old-fashioned-looking shops. I searched eagerly for a food store, but my heart sank with disappointment. There was a hardware store, where a very fat lady in dusty brown overalls

The shopkeepers stared at me

was standing outside, chatting to the ancient and skinny owner of a barber's shop next door.

On the opposite side were a toyshop and a television shop, but nothing selling food of any kind. The shopkeepers stared at me suspiciously, their noses sniffing and trembling in the air.

'What do you want?' enquired the lady in a rough squeak of a voice.

'Excuse me, I'm looking for something to eat,' I said.

'Well you won't find anything around here,' she replied, her plump cheeks wobbling like pink jellies.

'That's right, so 'op it!' cried the barber, his wrinkled face creasing into such a scowl it looked like a ball of scrunched-up paper. Then, grabbing a broom from inside his shop doorway, he thrust it towards me, walloping me in the chest.

'Hey!' I cried. 'What did you do that for?'

'We don't want Outcasts around here,' said the barber.

'I'm not an Outcast,' I protested. 'I don't even know what one is.'

'Well you look like one, you scruffy devil,' sniffed the man. 'Be off with you before we call a Guardian.'

'Yes, clear off, urchin,' said the fat lady, and she and the barber advanced towards me. A dapper little mouse-like man with a curling moustache came hurrying to join them, and together they herded me out of the courtyard into another alleyway.

'And don't come back,' yelled the barber as he gave me a parting whack with his broom.

I scurried along the rat-run of passages feeling shaken and very alone. Why was everyone so unfriendly? I hadn't done them any harm.

whack!

A Friendly Face

As the dim passage opened into another square, the clamour and bright colours of a bustling market momentarily dazzled me. People were swarming around the stalls, inspecting the goods and bartering noisily.

The market sold all sorts of things; clothes and shoes, picture frames and mobile phones, but the only one that caught my eye was the stall that displayed basket upon basket of red, shiny apples and ripe golden pears. I jangled the few coins in my pocket that 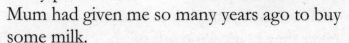 Mum had given me so many years ago to buy some milk.

As I stood watching the busy scene, I became aware that someone was scrutinizing me. It was a small, wiry boy and he was leaning against a wall on the other side of the square. His hands were thrust deep into the pockets of a long, tatty coat, and he was staring at me intently.

He saw me notice him and pushed himself

away from the wall and sauntered over.

'Watch yer,' he said as he approached, and gave me a wide grin. He was about ten or eleven years old with narrow shoulders and a skinny frame. He had the same pointed face as the rest of the inhabitants of Fortune City; a thatch of coarse hair was swept back from a low brow and he had sharp, protruding teeth that he sucked noisily. His clothes were dirty and frayed and he had a pinched, careworn look about him. 'You're new around 'ere, aren't yer?' he asked.

'Yes, I just arrived today,' I said. 'My name's Charlie; Charlie Small.'

'Pleased to meet you, Charlie, I'm sure,' said the friendly boy, thrusting a dirty hand out to shake mine. 'I'm Snipe. You look hungry, Charlie.'

'I'm starving,' I said. 'I haven't eaten for a couple of days.'

'That's no good. Follow me,' said Snipe with a friendly smile. 'I'll see yer all right.'

He was about ten or eleven years old

Snipe turned and pushed into the busy crowd of shoppers. 'C'mon; keep up,' he said over his shoulder.

I followed him across to the fruit stall, glad at last to have made a friend. Then I watched in horror as Snipe, standing behind the queue of people waiting to be served, carefully wormed his skinny arm between two chubby ladies. He grabbed a large apple from a basket, pulled his arm back and dropped the contraband into his pocket!

He turned and gave me a wink, but his self-satisfied smile turned to a look of shock as an arm darted from the crowd and grabbed him by the collar.

'Whoa!' cried Snipe as he was yanked backwards into the arms of a greasy-haired, mean-looking man. He was wearing a long, grey coat with wide, braided shoulders, and was balancing

on one of the single-wheeled mopeds I'd seen earlier.

'Got you, you pilfering pest,' growled the man, his thin lips curling back over his front teeth. 'You're coming with me.' I stepped forward to try and help, but Snipe's eyes flashed wide in warning, as if to say, *stay put*. Then the burly man, tottering on his unimoped, pushed Snipe through the crowd before him and I stood and stared stupidly, as they disappeared from view. Glancing around to check no one was watching me, I left the square by another narrow alleyway. *Typical*, I thought. *The only friendly person I've met since leaving Hawksmoor Hall, and he gets nabbed for pilfering!*

An Offer Of Help I Didn't Want!

I wandered along in a daze, wondering how I could find out where Snipe had been taken and if I should try to rescue him. Then, not looking where I was going, I accidentally whacked my shin against a signboard standing in the middle of the street.

'Ouch! What a stupid place to leave a . . . ' I

started to shout, but then stopped as I saw what the sign said:

'Brilliant!' I looked up at a wide-fronted shop, its windows full of bread, cheeses, pickle-jars, eggs, chocolate and sweets. My tummy rumbled in anticipation.

FAST FOOD

for workers in a **HURRY.**
Any **sandwich** made in **MINUTES.**

I barged into the shop. It was dim and dusty inside with lines of salamis and hams hanging from beams in the low ceiling. Tins of soup and jars of jam lined the shelves behind the counter and were stacked in neat pyramids on the floor. Behind the counter stood a short-sighted mole-like man, who peered at me through the gloom.

'A double-decker cheese, ham and gherkin torpedo roll, please,' I blurted, before the little bell over the door had even stopped ringing.

'Certainly, sir,' snuffled the short-sighted assistant and set straight to work. As I waited, the bell on the door rang again, but I was too enthralled watching the little man cut slices of crumbly cheese to bother turning round.

The smells in the shop were delicious. Rich, spicy and fruity aromas mingled in the air, making my mouth water and my stomach gurgle like a drain. The sixty-second wait was a terrible torture, and I nearly hopped over the counter and snatched the roll from his hands! Finally he was done.

'Fifteen gilpens,' he said, placing my sandwich on the counter.

The shopKeeper

'Gilpens?' I said stupidly. *Darn it!* It hadn't occurred to me that these people would have their own sort of money.

'That's right, fifteen gilpens,' the man repeated, his thin moustache twitching impatiently under his long nose.

'Is this any good?' I asked, placing my two pounds and fifty pence on the counter and making a grab for the torpedo roll. I wasn't quick enough! The man's hand slammed down on the roll like a trap.

'Fifteen gilpens,' he said for a third time, pushing my coins to one side with his other hand.

'But I'm starving!' I cried. 'Please, let me pay by doing the washing up or something.'

'Are you mad?' gasped the man. 'Not pay in cash? Fortune City would grind to a halt. It's fifteen gilpens or no food.' He was just about to take my lovely, fat torpedo roll away, when the customer standing behind me spoke up.

'Let him have it,' said a deep, rasping voice that sounded somehow familiar, and a rough hand reached over my shoulder and placed a coin on the counter.

'Oh, thanks mister, that's really kind,' I said, turning around. 'I haven't eaten for . . .' but there the words stuck in my throat. For looming over me like a cadaverous crow was Joseph Craik, the murderous thief-taker and my arch-enemy. He had vowed to see me hang and was determined to have my precious map. I almost fainted with shock.

It was Joseph Craik!

'Oh no!' I managed to croak, as a shiver of fear ran down my spine like icy water. I could hardly believe my eyes.

'So, we meet again, Charlie Small,' said Craik softly and menacingly. His one good eye stared coldly at me from a stony face.

I tried to make a bolt for the door but my legs had turned to jelly and the ruffian grabbed my shoulder in a powerful grip and hauled me back.

'What's the hurry, Charlie; don't you want your grub?' he asked calmly as his fingers dug painfully into my shoulder. He took the roll from the counter and stuffed it into one of his cavernous pockets.

'Let go, you're hurting!' I gasped.

'Excuse me,' said the shopkeeper nervously, but Craik ignored us both and steered me roughly towards the door. We were halfway out of the shop when the assistant called out again.

'Excuse me, sir. Your change,' he squeaked.

'Keep it, curse you,' barked Craik, turning angrily towards the man. As he did so, I managed to twist round, grab the door handle and slam the door shut on the bully's hand.

'*Yeeargh!*' bellowed Craik, letting go of me, and I pelted down the alley as fast as my legs could carry me.

Seconds later, Craik was out of the shop and after me. 'Gimme that map, boy,' he yelled in a cracked and rasping voice. 'Give it me, or I'll tear you apart like an overcooked chicken.'

I kept on running, my heart pounding with fear. I knew exactly why Craik wanted my map. He would find the route into my world, carry out the most daring robberies in the history of crime, and then escape back to the safety of his own world. That *must* not happen – it would be a disaster!

Clear off Craik!

Cornered

I had a head start on Craik, but I was exhausted and weak through lack of food. I turned down alleyway after alleyway, some deserted and others busy with shoppers, but Craik soon caught up with me. I could hear his rasping breath. His shadow fell across my path; I felt a tug on my sweatshirt, but I twisted free and ran round a corner. I knew Craik always carried a pistol, but surely it was too risky for him to use it in such a busy place?

Suddenly the vista changed. I raced across the main street again, and dived amongst a forest of massive columns that supported one of the glass skyscrapers. Weaving between them, I doubled back and hid behind a pillar deep in the shadows.

Craik's footsteps rang on the stone slabs, echoing from the ceiling of girders above. They stopped, started again and then slowly faded as the grasping old gangster hurried off in the wrong direction. I waited and waited until I was sure he had gone. Peeping from behind the pillar and seeing nothing amongst the shadows and shafts of light, I crept from beneath the towering building and turned into a street that ran along behind it.

Darn it, I thought, for I had walked into a quiet road at the back of a row of offices. The street sloped steeply up to a dead end, where a row of big, industrial wheelie bins was lined along the base of the high city wall.

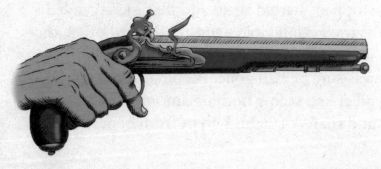

I was in a back road

Suddenly, with a banshee yell, Craik came careering after me from beneath the skyscraper.

'Ha! Got you cornered, you little creep,' he bellowed, as he stopped and drew his pistol. 'Now, give me that map.'

I backed along the street, desperately looking for an open door in the rear of the buildings, but they were all firmly closed.

'Come on, boy. It's time to give up; you're beaten,' sneered Craik, pacing towards me.

Nearly Nabbed!

'Leave me alone, Craik,' I said.

'Give me the map, and I promise I won't hurt you,' he said, pocketing his pistol and holding up his hands to show he was now unarmed. He took another step towards me.

'Not likely,' I said, but with the speed of a striking snake, Craik darted forward, grabbed my wrist and twisted my arm behind my back.

'*Yeargh!*' I yelled.

Craik's other arm snaked around my neck. 'Come on, hand it over, or I'll snap your arm like a twig,' he whispered in my ear.

'OK, OK! Just let me go,' I said. The creep released my aching arm and I pulled the map from my back pocket. Craik snatched the fold of paper from my grasp and ran his greedy eye over it.

'Oh, I'm getting close now, Charlie,' he sneered, licking his thin, scabby lips. 'Your world won't know what's hit it when I arrive.'

'You big creep,' I said, and then became aware of a low rumbling noise coming from the top of the slope. One of the big wheelie bins had started to roll down the hill, straight towards us.

I quickly stepped to one side but Craik was too busy studying the map to notice.

Come on, faster, faster, I said to myself, urging the bin on, for I could see it was on a collision course with the cretinous crook. At the last minute, Craik noticed the noise and whirled around in surprise. At the same time, the lid

A bin rumbled down the slope!

of the bin flipped open and the ratty head of a boy popped up. It was Snipe!

'I'll take that, thanks,' he cried, leaning forward and snatching the map from Craik's grasp. The bin whacked Craik hard on the shoulder and sent him flying. He landed with a sickening crack on the ground.

'Jump on,' yelled Snipe.

I ran full pelt, grabbed the lip of the bin and jumped up, finding a foothold on a small ledge that ran around the base. We rattled at ever increasing speed down the road as Craik got shakily to his feet and stumbled after us, clutching his shoulder.

'I'll get you. I'll get the pair of you!' he yelled, drawing his pistol and firing a shot into the air. 'And when I do, you'll be sorry.'

'So long, sucker!' I cried in delight. Then the bin hit a curb at the end of the road and tipped over. I was catapulted over the top and Snipe was thrown onto the pavement in a pile of decaying rubbish.

We jumped to our feet.

'Follow me,' cried Snipe and raced back under the skyscraper, flew across the main street and darted down a narrow alleyway.

Up To The Roof

Halfway down the alley, a metal fire-escape zig-zagged up the side of one of the buildings. The skinny boy leaped into the air, grabbed the bottom rung of a sliding ladder and pulled it to the ground.

'Quick, up you go,' he said, breathing hard. I looked over my shoulder and saw Craik limping across the main street. Clutching his injured shoulder, he loped towards our alley.

I raced up the rusting rungs and onto the first platform. Snipe followed and reached the top just as Craik appeared at the entrance to the passage. As Snipe stepped from the ladder it sprang up behind us with a noisy rattle.

'I can see yer,' growled Craik and raised his pistol and fired.

Ptang! The bullet ricocheted from the metal platform and the villain reached up to drag the ladder back down.

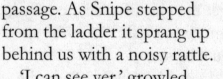

PTANG!

'No, yer don't,' cried Snipe and rammed a block of wood under one of the rungs, locking the ladder in place. 'C'mon,' he said to me again and we hurtled up a flight of iron stairs to the next platform, and then the next.

Ptang! Another bullet hit the metal grill beneath our feet, making it ring like a bell. We carried on climbing. Craik let off another volley. *Ptang!* Then we were at the top, and rolled over a low parapet onto the roof.

I looked cautiously over the wall, hoping to leave with a taunting remark, but Craik had already gone and I breathed a huge sigh of relief. Then I felt dizzy and had to sit down.

Snipe Again

Snipe sat down beside me, his back against the parapet.

'You all right, Charlie?' he asked.

'Just a bit wobbly,' I said, taking a few deep breaths.

'That's hunger, that is. 'Ere, you'd better 'ave this,' he said. He reached into a deep pocket in his dirty coat and took out my double-decker cheese, ham and gherkin torpedo roll.

'Where did you get that?' I cried.

'I lifted it from matey-boy's pocket when I whacked him with the bin,' said Snipe, smiling proudly.

That reminded me that I'd seen Snipe taken prisoner less than an hour before. 'Just a minute,' I said. 'How did you escape from that man?'

'Oh, that was nothin',' said Snipe with a grin. 'The City Guardians can't hold me. I'm as slippery as an eel, I am!'

'What's a City Guardian?' I asked as I ripped open the paper bag and bit off a large mouthful of roll.

I'm as slippery as an eel!

'A bloomin' nuisance is what they are,' said Snipe. 'They're a snoopin' police force that roams the streets, checkin' everyone is hard at work and doing what they're supposed to be doing.'

My torpedo roll was scrumptious, and before I knew it there was only a small piece left. 'Oh, sorry!' I said through a mouthful of bread. 'I forgot. Do you want some?'

'Nah, you're all right!' said Snipe, staring at the doughy bap that I held out. 'You finish . . . oh,' he added mournfully as I hungrily stuffed the last piece in my mouth. 'You already 'ave. Feelin' any better?'

'A bit,' I said. 'Thanks for rescuing me, by the way.'

'Think nothin' of it,' he replied, scratching at his front teeth with a long, dirty fingernail. 'I was wonderin' if I'd bump into you again. I was hidin' out in that wheelie bin when I saw you pelt round the corner, chased by that scar-faced goon. Who is he, anyway?'

'His name's Craik,' I said. 'He's after my map.'

'Oh yeah, I nearly forgot. You'd better 'ave it back,' said Snipe.

'Oh, brilliant!' I cried as I took my precious map. 'Do you realize how important this is?'

But Snipe didn't answer. He was staring up at the millions of blank windows in the skyscrapers that rose all around us. 'Come on, Charlie,' he said. 'It's time we got goin'. There's too many pryin' eyes round 'ere.'

I got to my feet, but I was still feeling woozy.

My head felt hot and little droplets of sweat popped out on my forehead as I staggered across the rooftop after Snipe. I felt as if I was in some sort of weird, swirling dream.

'Why's that map so important, then?' I heard Snipe ask, sounding a long way away. 'Is it a treasure map or somefing?'

'It's better than that. It shows a route into a parallel world and was made by the granddaughter of a nutty inventor called Jakeman,' I babbled, feverishly. 'He did a space and time continuum experiment that went wrong and dragged me from my world into this world, and he makes weird and wonderful mechanimals like the steam-powered rhinoceros, and I've been away from home for four hundred years and this is my only chance of getting back, and Craik wants my map, but he mustn't get it and . . . and . . .' And then I fainted.

The next thing I knew, my face was splashed with cold water and I opened my eyes. Snipe was kneeling beside me

I felt very hot
- and then I fainted

with my battered old water bottle in his hand.

'You'd better come 'ome with me and get some rest, Charlie. You was talkin' complete gobbledegook!' said Snipe. 'Come on, I'll 'elp yer up.'

He got me to my feet and we walked to the far side of the building, from where I could see a crowded roofscape of tiled ridges and valleys, steep gables and soaring towers stretching before me across the city.

We crossed a high metal gantry that spanned an alleyway below, onto the roof of the building next door. Here, a row of thick chimneys sprouted up like strange, branchless trees. We climbed between them and walked across a wobbly, narrow plank onto another roof. I was so light-headed that Snipe had to hold my hand to make sure I didn't tumble to the ground below.

Snipe's Hideout

We clambered up tiled slopes and between outcrops of twisted, leaning chimneys. We jumped narrow alleys, slid down copper-lined gullies and climbed up wobbling drainpipes until we eventually arrived at Snipe's home.

'Here we are,' said Snipe proudly as we climbed over a tall parapet that surrounded a wide, flat roof. 'Home sweet home!'

I don't know what I was expecting, but certainly not the untidy collection of dilapidated huts and makeshift tents that were hidden behind the walls. Sheets of a dark, meshed material had been stretched above the shelters. They were attached to wooden poles all around the parapet and acted as camouflage against prying eyes in a nearby skyscraper.

Five or six other raggedy children were
gathered in the shadows beneath the
camouflage. A short, dumpy, mouse-like woman
with no neck and grey, straggly hair was sifting
through a bag that one of the children had just
handed her. She was dressed in a dirty old skirt,
a stained apron and a long shawl, and looked
like a walking pile of jumble.

'You've done well, Tips. That's a nice haul of
silver spoons. We can melt them down and sell
the silver,' she was saying.

'Cooeee!' cried Snipe
as we approached, and
the woman looked up
sharply.

'Who's with you,
Snipe?' she asked
suspiciously, her
nose twitching
nervously in
the air.

'It's all right. He's
a friend,' said Snipe.
'He was in a bit of
bother and needed
some help.'

Who's your friend?

'You sure he can be trusted?' asked the woman.

'Yeah, he's on the run, like us,' said Snipe.

She stared at me with her dark, tiny round eyes. 'OK, I believe you,' she said. 'He looks worn out. Take him to your hut and I'll bring some food over in a minute.'

My new friend led me to a shabby hut near the wall. It was dim, dirty and draughty inside, but there was a trestle bed along one wall, with a pile of blankets on top.

'There y'are,' said Snipe. 'You can use my bed. I've got an old mattress somewhere I can use.'

I didn't need to be told twice. I let my rucksack fall to the ground, stretched out on the sagging bed and was asleep in seconds.

Mrs Mudge

When I woke up the next morning, I was on my own. The thin mattress that Snipe had slept on was rolled up and stuffed in a corner, but he'd left a grubby note on my pillow that read:

Gone foragin'.
Be back later,
Snipe
P.S. Don't touch nuthin'.

'What's *foragin*' when it's at home?' I muttered to myself, and lay back on my pillow. I was still feeling worn out after my adventures but, stretching and yawning, I made myself get up.

The little shed that Snipe called home was like an old junk shop, piled high with all sorts of curiosities. There was a stack of mouldy books with a flowerpot on top in which grew a single dandelion. There was an old drum, its skin torn open with a bird's nest resting inside. A stack of cardboard boxes contained a collection of broken toys, and an old-fashioned watch on a chain hung from a ceiling joist.

On a narrow shelf around the whole of the inside of the shed stood a display of chipped plates and bowls and empty picture frames. Pinned to the wall above the head of the bed was a small grubby newspaper clipping, with a faded photograph of a very self-satisfied rat-faced man. The heading above, read: Mr Grindstone, Fortune City Employee Of The Month – Again!

Mr Grindstone, Fortune City Employee Of The Month – Again!

I crept over to the open shed door and peered out. In the middle of the roof was the woman I had seen the previous evening. She was stirring something in a large pot but looked up sharply as I stuck my head out. I quickly drew it back in, but she had spotted me.

'You must be starving, dearie,' she called out. 'You were fast asleep when I brought you your grub last night.'

My tummy rumbled and I stepped outside. There was a bright sun in a clear sky, but the camouflage net above us cast a mottled shadow over the grey roof.

'I haven't eaten for ages,' I said. 'Well, only a roll.'

'Come on then, Charlie Small,' said the woman. 'There's always food on the go here.'

'You know my name,' I said as I joined her at the black pot that stood bubbling over the glowing embers of a fire.

'Snipe told me,' she said, ladling out a bowlful of baked beans and stew. 'And you can call me Mrs Mudge, seein' as that's *my* name.'

Baked bean and leftover stew

'Pleased to meet you, Mrs Mudge,' I said, tipping a spoonful of beans into my mouth. She had a slightly bossy, no nonsense air about her, but seemed very kind and I immediately started to relax. 'Mmmm, that's lovely!'

I scoffed my food down in seconds. Mrs Mudge smiled and spooned out another bowl. I scoffed that down too, and then held my bowl out for thirds, but she shook her head.

'You want to take it easy, young man,' she said. 'You'll be giving yourself stomach ache at this rate.' Then, pointing to a wide gully that ran along one side of the roof, she added, 'Washing up goes in the gutter. Just pull that chain on the side of the tank, Charlie.'

I went over and placed my bowl in the trough. On a brick plinth was a large, metal tank that supplied water to the apartments in the building below. I pulled a short chain and water gushed from a pipe and cascaded along the gutter. I rinsed my bowl quickly before the water gurgled away down a drainpipe, and then stood it to dry in a patch of sunlight.

'Where is everybody?' I asked.

'They're, um . . . just collecting,' said Mrs Mudge.

'Collecting what?' I asked. Had Snipe been 'just collecting' apples when he was nabbed in the square?

'Oh, I haven't got time for a lot of questions, Charlie Small,' said Mrs Mudge, sitting on a low wall and dragging a sack of old clothes between her feet. 'I've got my sorting to do, dearie, and can't stand around gossiping all day. You must try to amuse yourself. The others will be back at lunch time.'

There wasn't much to amuse myself with on the rooftop. Snipe had forbidden me to touch his precious possessions, and there's only so much fun I could have by folding paper boats from old newspapers and making them ride the rapids as I sent a tide of water gushing along the gutter. So I've spent the rest of the time bringing my journal up to date.

I'm going to stop now, because some of the children I saw yesterday are reappearing. I'll write more later.

The Set-up

They arrived in ones and twos; shinning up
drainpipes, popping out of skylights and
squeezing between tall, terracotta chimneypots.
Snipe was one of the first back and as soon as he
had deposited an old canvas bag at Mrs Mudge's
feet and received a bowl of food in return, he
came hurrying over.

'How's it going, Charlie? You feeling any
better?' asked Snipe, twitching his long nose.

'Much better, thanks,' I said.

'Good for you,' said the boy. Then, looking at
me more seriously he added, 'I suppose you're
wonderin' what we've been up to all day.'

'I can sort of guess,' I said.

'Well, sit down anyway, Charlie, and let me tell
it like it is,' he said, and I sat on a low chimney
pot that felt nice and warm beneath me.

'Every day our little gang goes out, scourin'
the city for anything useful,' began Snipe.
'Whatever we find, we bring back to Mrs Mudge.
She's the organizer; she tells us what we need
and sorts through our haul, separatin' anything
edible from stuff that can be used in our camp,
and other things that need to be sold on.'

'When you say *find*, what exactly do you mean?' I asked.

'Just that, *find*,' said Snipe. 'We might find somethin' in someone's pocket, or on a sill by an open window. Sometimes if we have to, we find things in shops. Mrs Mudge gives us our daily tasks while she stays in camp preparin' our meals and tidyin' up the huts.'

Oh heck, I thought. *I've landed in a proper little thieves' kitchen!*

'Now you know our set-up, it's about time you met the others,' continued Snipe. 'Come and meet Charlie,' he yelled. 'The latest member of our gang.'

We might find something by an open window

The others took up their bowls and hurried over, all shouting and talking good-humouredly at once. Their names are Tips, Talia, Finn, Midge and Snotty, and they instantly made me feel very welcome.

'How did you get here?' asked Talia, a nervous, stick-thin girl with the palest face I've ever seen.

'I came across the wasteland on a hovering scooter,' I replied. 'But it turned into a sea halfway across.'

'Oh, it does that,' said Snipe. 'For six months of the year it's a desert, but then water boils up from the porous rocks below and it becomes an ocean for the other six months. You must've got caught in the changeover. You're lucky to be alive!'

'Where do you come from?' asked Midge, a stocky boy with a rash of brown freckles on his pointed face.

'From another world, entirely,' I replied.

'Is dat why you've got such a stubby-dosed face?' asked Snotty, wiping his blocked and runny nose on the back of his hand.

'Who are you on the run from, Charlie?' asked Finn.

Snotty   Talia

'Quiet down and don't crowd him,' cried Snipe. 'He might not want to tell us.'

'It's all right,' I said, and told Snipe and his friends all about my many adventures. I told them how I've been trying to get home for four hundred years, and why Craik is after my map.

'He's been my enemy ever since I was a member of a gang of cut-throat pirates. I robbed him and sunk his galleon,' I explained. 'Then, when he found out I came from a different world and had a map showing me how to get back there, he became obsessed with taking it. Once he knows where the portal between the two worlds is situated, he plans on passing through, performing a series of dastardly crimes and then making a safe getaway back into this world.'

Snipe didn't seem at all interested or surprised that I came from a completely different world. 'Well, I didn't think you came from round here with a snub-nosed fizzog like yours,' he laughed. But he was impressed with Craik's plan. 'Wow, cool!' he said with a whistle. Then, seeing my shocked expression he quickly added, 'No, what I mean is, *how dreadful*!'

My face fell. Snipe and his pals were so

friendly I had forgotten that they were thieves too!

'Don't worry, Charlie,' said Snipe with a grin. 'We don't want your map. We only steal things in order to survive. We are Outcasts, not outlaws!'

'Outcasts? What do you mean?' I asked.

The Outcasts

We're no angels!

'We're no angels, that's for sure,' said Snipe. 'But we ain't rogues either. Look, it's like this. Fortune City is a big, unforgivin' machine; a machine of offices and factories and shops, and it needs all those mugs you saw buzzin' about like flies to keep it going. If one part stops, the whole city will grind to a halt. Then what would everybody do?'

'I dunno,' I said, shrugging my shoulders.

'Neither do they, that's the problem,' said Snipe. 'Well, me and my mates are cogs that don't fit into the machine, and there's plenty more of us all over the city, young and old. We don't want to spend our lives shut up in a tall tower block, pressin' buttons and sortin' paper. It's a mug's game! So, we survive the only way we can. I forage and pick the odd pocket. Nothing big, and it's a fine life once you get used to it. It's what is called a lifestyle choice, Charlie, and I've chosen the life of an Outcast!'

'It's stealing!' I said. 'It's wrong. You wouldn't like it if somebody took your stuff.'

'That's pretty strong, coming from someone who used to be a rampagin' pirate,' said Snipe, not the least bit offended. 'Anyway, I haven't got nothin' worth stealin'. Ha!' he added, and folded his arms in triumph, convinced he'd won the argument.

'Where are your mums and dads?' I asked, changing the subject.

'Mudge *is* our ma,' said Tips, a girl with cropped hair, startling violet eyes, and the youngest of the gang. 'Our dad was a City messenger, but he faded away from exhaustion a couple of years ago.'

ARR! I used to be a pirate!

'Dat's why we decided do become Outcasts,' sniffed Snotty, wiping his nose and leaving a gooey trail on his sleeve. 'We ain't going the same way as Pops.'

'Oh, I'm sorry,' I said. 'Is Mrs Mudge your mum too?' I asked Snipe.

'Nah! My folks are still around somewhere beaverin' away in one of these skyscrapers, trying to stay Employee of the Month,' he said. 'I hardly ever used to see 'em, though; they were always workin'. So one day I decided to clear out and live on my wits.'

'Won't they be worried?' I asked, shocked.

'Probably haven't even noticed,' he replied quietly and a sad look flickered across his face. 'Anyway, enough of this; who's for some more grub?'

'You bet,' cried the rest of the gang. 'Dish it out, Snipe!'

The Next Day

The gang was out all day today. I helped Mrs Mudge sort through yesterday's haul and file away some engraved initials on a silver ladle.

The Day After That

Gradually getting my strength
back. Snotty brought
back a massive roast
turkey today, still hot
from an oven. It was
delicious, but goodness
knows where he managed
to get it, or how he
carried it home through the swarming streets!

The Following Day

I had tummy ache all day from eating too much
turkey!

A Few Days Later

It's the end of another day and I'm tucked up
in bed, writing my journal. I've been with the
Outcasts for about a week now, and I'm starting
to feel my old self again. I've been well fed and
made really welcome by the whole gang, even

Mrs Mudge, who fusses around us all like an old mother hen.

It's strange living on the roof of a building, but there is plenty of space and some wonderful views over the city. One of the skyscrapers looks down on our camp, but the camouflage sheets keep us well hidden. The smoke from Mrs Mudge's cooking isn't spotted as it gets mixed up with the steam and smoke that billows from the chimneystacks and flues that sprout all over our roof.

The Outcasts go collecting every day, and while they're away I either help Mrs Mudge around the camp or sit, leaning against a warm chimneystack, reading one of the books that the gang have brought back for me.

Sometimes the Outcasts come back with their canvas bags full of food and bric-a-brac, sometimes with hardly anything at all. Now and again one of the gang gets chased by the City Guardians, but they never venture up onto the roofs and we all feel quite safe, hidden amongst the smoke and the chimneys.

Whilst he's been out, Snipe has been scouring the city for any news of Craik, but he hasn't had sight or sound of him. He's visited some of the other Outcast camps, but they haven't seen him either.

'But how would they know? They don't know what he looks like,' I said.

'They'd know him, Charlie. He's a flat-face like you. The pair of you stick out like sore thumbs in this place,' laughed Snipe.

I wonder if Craik has finally given up his hunt for me, and left Fortune City.

My journal is right up to date now, and it's time I thought about moving on. But, before I can leave Fortune City, there's something I have to do. This evening, as Snipe and I were chatting away in his tumbledown shed, Mrs Mudge poked her wrinkled and careworn face round the door.

'Ready for bed, you two?' she asked. 'Good lads. Well, Charlie, you've been here a week now, and although it's been a pleasure and I don't begrudge you a thing, the Outcasts have a rule. Only one rule, but a rule nonetheless. *Everyone* who stays with us must contribute to the gang, dearie! Tomorrow, I want you to go out with Snipe and see what you can pick up. Goodnight boys!'

'Don't worry, Charlie,' said Snipe, seeing my

Everyone must contribute to the gang, dearie!

worried expression. 'I'll show you the ropes.'

Oh, heck! What will I have to do?

I've been trying to get to sleep for ages now, but I'm way too nervous about tomorrow. Snipe's not worried. It's just another working day for him, and he's already fast asleep on his mattress on the floor, snoring noisily and grinding his big, buck teeth.

I'll write more later.

Oh, heck! What have I let myself in for?

Foraging

'What *is* foraging?' I asked the next morning. 'If it involves picking any pockets you can count me out. My pirate raids nearly ended up with me swinging on the gallows, and I don't want to risk that again.'

'Don't worry, Charlie,' said Snipe. 'All we're gonna do is find a full waste bin and take anything that's edible. We do it all the time.'

'But the food will be rotten,' I said.

'Not at all,' explained my friend as I followed him across the roof. 'Fortune City produces so much food that they dump anything that's not absolutely perfect. Bananas have to be the right shape. Tomatoes have to be perfectly round and bread just the right shade of golden brown. Anything that doesn't come up to scratch gets dumped.'

This one is too bent!

'That's crazy. What a waste!' I cried. 'No one can complain about us helping ourselves to *that*.'

'You'd think so, wouldn't you?' said Snipe.

'But I'm not gonna kid you, Charlie. Even though they're just going to trash the food, it's still against the law for someone to raid a waste bin in Fortune City. If we get caught, we'll be up before the beak!'

'Oh, great!' I said.

We slid down a drainpipe onto a lower roof, scampered across and climbed down a set of concrete steps into a small backyard, behind a building on a street corner. Snipe opened a high wooden gate and we walked out into a bustling lane.

'Keep close and follow me,' said Snipe as we were pushed and jostled by the moving crowd. 'If we get separated in this lot, we'll never find each other again.'

I kept as close as I could to the boy as he rapidly wriggled his way through the mass of bodies, crossing the street and turning off down another side road. We turned left and right and right again, until I was completely bewildered and had no idea where we were. Finally, we turned down a street behind a giant food store where tall bins were lined up in a yard, outside some big, swing doors.

'Here we are, Charlie,' said Snipe, handing

me a large hessian bag. 'I'll climb into a bin and chuck the food down to you.'

We darted across the yard and, with a couple of practised jumps, Snipe scaled the smooth side of the first bin and sat precariously on top.

'Keep an eye out for the City Guardians,' he said. 'You can't miss 'em. They all look like the one that nabbed me. They wear grey coats and ride those motorized unicycles.' With that, he dropped down inside the bin.

I looked around nervously, my heart starting to bang against my chest, but the courtyard remained quiet and deserted.

'Open the bag, Charlie.' Snipe's booming voice echoed from inside, and I held out the bag as a stream of food started flying out of the top of the bin. I scuttled back and forth, catching the food in the bag as it rained down; a burnt loaf of bread, a limp lettuce, a bag of knobbly potatoes and an old cabbage.

Then Snipe clambered out and leaped into the next bin along. More food started to fly through the air and I began to enjoy myself, running to catch the flying items in my bag. That's probably why I didn't hear the *putt-putt-putt* of approaching motors until it was too late.

I whirled round as two Guardians on unimopeds buzzed into the yard.

Fortune City Guardians

'Uh-oh, we've got company,' I said softly. 'Guardians!'

'How many?' asked Snipe in an echoing whisper.

'Two, and they don't look very friendly,' I said. The heavy-set men had slicked-back hair and wore dark glasses that hid their eyes. Their

long, braided coats almost touched the ground and hid all but the bottom half of the wheels of their mopeds, making it look as if they were hovering over the ground.

The men came towards me. 'Stay right where you are, sonny,' said one, taking a notebook and pencil from his coat. 'Right, what's your name and what do you think you're playin' at?'

'I, um, I. Well, I,' I said, totally lost for words as my legs started to shake.

'Come on, spit it out. What are you hanging around the bins for? That's City property, you know,' he continued. 'Let's have a look in your bag. If you've been pilfering, you'll find yourself in serious trouble.'

'I haven't, honest,' I said. 'Look, I'd better get going; I'm expected at home.'

'Freeze!' barked the Guardian. 'Or I'll zap you with my stun gun!' And he pulled out a scary-looking weapon shaped like an angry shark.

The stun gun was shaped like a shark!

'Not seen one before?' he said with a sneer. 'Then let me inform you that this little baby sends out an invisible beam that can freeze a person like stone for up to ten minutes.'

'By which time we have them cuffed and on the way to the cells,' boasted the other man. 'Neat, eh?'

'Hello,' said Snipe, popping his head out of the bin.

'*You!*' cried the Guardian. 'I might have known it. Right, stay exactly where you are.'

'*Get down* from there,' said the other one at exactly the same time.

'What do you want me to do: get down or stay put?' said Snipe, cheekily.

'Get down!' they both shouted at the same time.

Snipe climbed onto the edge of the bin. He had a big, squashy, rotting cabbage in each hand and, as he leaped from the bin he pelted one and then the other at the Guardians.

Splat! Splodge! They landed smack in the men's faces. They toppled backwards and their unimopeds landed with a satisfying crash on the ground. The motors spluttered and stopped.

'Run!' cried Snipe and we scarpered across the

yard. The two Guardians tried to kick-start their mopeds, but the machines coughed and died, so they came after us on foot. *Oh, yikes!*

I spun round, pulling the bag of marbles from my rucksack at the same time, and sent them rolling over the ground into the men's path.

'*Whoa!*' they yelled as they went skidding and sliding on the little glass balls, their legs going in opposite directions. But still they kept coming, like very bad skaters on a frozen pond. One of the Guardians reached clumsily out to grab me when, *thump!* His partner went down.

'Ooof!' he groaned as he hit the ground, and *POW!* His stun gun went off and the invisible beam hit his pal.

'Got y . . .' was all the man managed to say before he was frozen solid.

The Guardian was turned as solid as stone!

'See you later,' cried Snipe as we shinned up a drainpipe and went hell for leather over the rooftops. We didn't stop until we arrived back at Snipe's camp.

Some Unwelcome News

'It was a close one, Mrs Mudge,' said Snipe as we handed her our bag of comestible contraband. 'Charlie was a star, though. I'm not surprised he made such a good pirate.'

'Well done, Charlie,' said Mrs Mudge, smiling.

'What happened?' cried Talia as all the others crowded round to hear Snipe tell our story. He embellished and embroidered it to such an extent that even I was amazed at how brave I'd been!

'The snarlin' Guardians came at us like rabid watchdogs, but Charlie bravely stood his ground,' he said. 'He waited and waited until the very last minute before lettin' go with his marbles. He must have calculated *just* where to roll 'em, because when one Guardian went down, he shot the other and froze him in mid-leap. It was spectacular!'

'Oh, neat!' cried the Outcasts.
'Bravo, Charlie!' It was such a
good story I didn't like to tell
them it had been pure luck!

'You'll be a marked man
now, though,' Mrs Mudge told me. 'You'd better
stay in camp for a bit.'

So I spent the rest of the day relaxing in
Snipe's hut, sprawled out on the trestle bed,
reading old Fortune City newspapers. I found
this report that mentions the Outcasts:

Just before bedtime, when we were chatting
around the stewpot, Finn came back from an
expedition with some bad news.

'You're famous, Charlie,' he said with a grin.
'There are 'Wanted!' posters of you all over the
City!'

'You're joking,' I said.

'Am I?' he replied, and pulled a folded bit of
paper from his back pocket. 'It's a bit torn. It
was on a telegraph pole and I had to rip it down
quick, without being seen. It's against the law to
remove City property.'

I unfolded it and stared at a blurred,
photocopied image of me under the heading:

A Threat To Increased Production

'Congratulations to all our citizens. Fortune City is running like a well-oiled machine,' the City Fathers said today. But they also warned that the number of Outcasts in our City is growing all the time. 'This cannot be allowed to continue,' they said.

Only last week, a gang of Outcasts led by a skinny mastermind called Snipe raided the City Soup Factory. They drilled a small hole in a soup tank, inserted a tube and siphoned some off for their own use.

'This is a despicable misuse of City property,' said a spokesperson. 'Outcasts are a drain on our City, and Snipe is the worst of all. The City Guardians have been after this pesky pickpocket for a long time.'

If you have any information as to his whereabouts, please report to the nearest Guardian. Keep your eyes peeled and your shoulders to the wheel, citizens. Remember! We are all cogs in the machine!

Snipe

WANTED! The Flat-faced Outcast who foiled City Guardians.

'Oh, not again,' I moaned. I've been on posters before, when I was the most wanted pirate on the high seas. But this was different. 'Where the heck did they get that photo?' I asked.

'Oh, dere's CCTV cameras all over de City,' said Snotty, wiping his nose on a dirty rag and sniffing loudly. 'Dey can take a picture, print off a poster and ged it posted all over town within half an hour.'

'Welcome to the Outcasts!' said Mrs Mudge.

Making Plans

'If you're serious about gettin' home, I wouldn't hang around too long,' said Snipe. 'If you get pulled in for the waste bin caper, you might not see daylight for a year.'

'What are you on about?' I exclaimed. I didn't like the sound of this one bit.

'That's the amount of time you'll get in the Hole if you're caught,' said Snipe. 'We've all done a stretch.'

'The Hole?' I gulped.

'Yeah, that's what the City prison is called. You don't want to get sent to the Hole,' said Midge with a shudder. 'It's dark and creepy and full of spiders.'

Welcome to The Hole!

'And de grub is terrible, *sniff*,' said Snotty.

'I'll go first thing in the morning,' I said. There was no way I wanted to end up in that grim-sounding place. 'But I've lost my Air-rider with its GPS device. Can you tell me the best direction to take?'

'Let's have a look at that map again,' said Snipe.

I handed over the map and he studied it for a few minutes.

'Well, if we can swing it, the answer is staring us in the face,' he said. 'You can take the train!'

Of course! Why hadn't it occurred to me before? There was a railway track marked on the map, leading from Fortune City to within a few kilometres of the wood I was heading for.

'Excellent!' I said. 'So what's the problem?'

'Well, first of all, you are Wanted. The Guardians are bound to be lookin' for you, so you'll have to be disguised,' explained Snipe. 'And secondly, train tickets cost money and we haven't got any. So we'll have to go dippin' for the funds.'

'Dipping?' I asked, starting to feel very uneasy.

'We'll 'ave to pick a pocket or two,' grinned Snipe.

'No way!' I exclaimed.

'There will be lookouts posted at the City gates. They might have even locked them. The train is your only chance,' said Snipe. 'It's what's called a moral dilemma, Charlie!'

I'm lying in the trestle bed, ready for sleep, and Snipe is curled up on his old mattress on the floor, snoring through his twitching, elongated nose. My journal is bang up to date and I'm ready to leave first thing in the morning. Mrs Mudge is going to see to my disguise and Snipe is going to see me on to the train. I don't like the idea of picking a pocket, but Snipe says we've got no choice. What would you do?

I'll write more later.

I've got myself in a terrible bind!

You've Got To Pick A Pocket Or Two

'Your own muvver wouldn't recognize yer,' laughed Snipe.

I looked in the shard of mirror that Mrs Mudge handed me and studied my disguise. She'd done a pretty good job.

She'd taken one of those old fashioned cardboard party hats, shaped like a cone, and painted it the same colour as my skin. She cut some holes in it, for nostrils, and darkened the tip to match their own rodent-like noses. I stretched the elastic strap round the back of my

Bushy eyebrows

False nose and teeth

Padding

head and placed the cone over my mouth and nose. Next, Mrs Mudge stuck some false, hairy eyebrows on top of my own, greased my hair and brushed it back. Then she found a smart overcoat for me to wear, which we padded out with some cushions to make me appear fatter.

'You look just like one of the chubby workers that scuttle about the streets,' giggled Snipe.

'Well, that's all I can do,' said Mrs Mudge, standing back and admiring her handiwork. 'You'd better get going, boys. Good luck and *bon voyage,* Charlie dearie. It's been a pleasure knowing you.'

'Bye, everyone,' I called to the Outcasts, as I got ready to follow Snipe down a drainpipe to the next level of roofs. 'Thanks for everything. Bye!'

We were soon at ground level. Old stone

buildings loomed over us on each side, and behind those the glass office towers soared up into a perfect, blue sky. It was a beautiful morning. I just hope it doesn't end with us being thrown in the Hole!

Snipe led me through a maze of narrow streets, crowded with people. We had to be extra vigilant, because Snipe was Wanted too, but he was an expert at blending in with the crowd and kept a sharp lookout for any roving Guardians. The strange little people were so intent on getting to work, they didn't give us a second glance. My makeshift disguise seemed to be working!

'Right, keep your wits about yer. It's time to go to work,' said Snipe as we entered a broad forecourt, surrounded on three sides by shops. The concourse was milling with people all heading to and from a wide arch in a long white building on the opposite side – the Railway Station. I immediately became nervous and started to sweat under the thick padding around my chest and tummy.

'It's the perfect spot,' said Snipe. 'Keep right behind me, Charlie,' and with that he dived deeper into the mass of moving bodies. We pushed our way through them and then, with a quick look around, Snipe thrust his hand into the pocket of the man in front of him. I held my breath, praying that the man wouldn't feel anything. Then Snipe removed his hand and shook his head. 'Empty!' he whispered. We let ourselves be carried along by the tide of people and then Snipe tried his luck again.

In went his hand, his fingers expertly lifting the pocket's flap and then delving inside. This time Snipe extracted a handful of gilpens and we quickly turned and pushed ourselves towards the edge of the crowd. Standing in the recess of a doorway, Snipe counted his haul.

'Flip!' he said. 'I've come up light. We're gonna 'ave to try again, Charlie m'boy.'

'Are you sure?' I asked, because my heart was beating fit to burst, and I was feeling terrible about taking someone else's stuff.

'Got no choice, Charlie. You're gonna need double this amount,' said my friend. 'I don't usually like dipping more than twice in one area. It's askin' for trouble. But we'll give it one more go.'

Again we pushed into the crowd, forcing our way to the middle until people were squashed all around us. We found ourselves behind a person in a blue coat with bulging pockets and Snipe gave me the nod.

Just a minute, that man's a lot taller than the rest of the crowd, I thought, feeling uneasy as Snipe dipped his hand into the target's pocket. A grin spread across Snipe's face and, giving me a wink, he pulled out a leather bag that jingled with coins. But just as we turned to leave, the man span around. He grabbed Snipe's wrist with a bandaged hand, scattering the coins on the ground amongst the crowd's rushing feet.

'A dipper!' snarled the man. 'I'll wring your scrawny neck, you thievin' little magpie.'

Oh, heck! Of all the people in Fortune City to try and rob, Snipe had found JOSEPH CRAIK!

Taking The A-Train

'I've caught a thief,' bellowed Craik, his hand clamped tightly around Snipe's skinny arm. 'I've nabbed a pilfering pickpocket!'

The swarm of people slowed down, staring at Snipe as he struggled in the tall man's grip, but they didn't stop.

'Sorry; can't stop or we'll be late for work,' said a short, snuffling man.

'Hand him over to a Guardian,' said another, hurrying by. 'Look – here comes one now.'

Sure enough, the crowd was parting as a grey-coated Guardian motored across the wide concourse on his unimoped.

'Just a minute,' snarled Craik, staring more closely at Snipe. 'Don't I know you?'

'Run, Charlie!' yelled Snipe. 'Get away while you can!'

'Charlie?' snarled Craik, looking at me. 'It can't be Charlie Small!' He made a grab for me with his other hand. I managed to squirm out of the way, but my home-made mask was knocked askew.

'It *is* you,' sneered Craik, grabbing at me again as I was barged and buffeted by the crowd flowing past us. 'Give me that flamin' map, boy!'

You must be joking! I thought. I wasn't going to hang around to be carted off to the Hole whilst Craik disappeared with my map. I wasn't going to leave Snipe in the lurch either. I ran at Craik, ducked under his grasping hand and kicked him as hard as I could on the shin.

'Flamin' heck!' yelled Craik, letting go of Snipe, who kicked him hard on the other leg. 'Aaargh!' he screamed, and clutched his throbbing shins.

'Go, Snipe, go! I'll be all right,' I cried.

'I can't just leave yer,' said Snipe, as the sound of the Guardian's moped got nearer.

'Don't worry about me,' I said. 'Go, before you're hauled off to the Hole.'

'You sure?' asked the boy.

'Go!' I insisted. 'I'll get on the train somehow.'

Then, coming closer, he whispered in my ear. 'Take the A-Train, Charlie,' he said. 'And good luck!'

As the Guardian arrived on the scene, weaving his way through the hurrying throng, Snipe squeezed into the crowd and disappeared from view as if by magic. I pushed back into the moving multitude behind me. Nobody cried out, or dragged me kicking and screaming over to the Guardian; everyone was so intent on catching their train they didn't even seem to notice me squashed in amongst them, and I let myself be carried towards the Railway Station.

I was swept along, under the wide arch and into the City Station. To my right stood a row of gates, leading on to the platforms. To my left was a line of ticket offices, but they were no use as I had no money. I was going to have to try and board the train without a ticket.

I ran along the gates, peering up at the signs above.

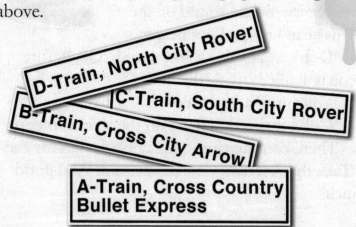

D-Train, North City Rover

C-Train, South City Rover

B-Train, Cross City Arrow

A-Train, Cross Country Bullet Express

That's it, the A-Train, I thought. *That's the one I want! Now, how the heck am I going to get on it?*

'All aboard,' shouted the man at the gate. 'The A-Train is about to depart. All aboard!'

'Excuse me, mister,' I said to the guard.

'Ticket, please,' he replied.

'I don't have a ticket, but I *really* need to get on that train. Couldn't I send you the fare later?'

'Travel without a ticket?' gasped the guard, his nose twitching violently and his face flushing a deep red. 'If we allowed people to do that, Fortune City would—'

'Grind to a halt!' I finished the sentence for him. Then a loud hissing noise came from the platform beyond the gate and the sleek, bullet-shaped train started to move forward.

'Too late now, anyway,' said the guard. Then, looking over my shoulder his face froze. 'Well I never,' he said, his eyes bulging like ping-pong balls. I turned round and saw the Wanted! poster with my blooming photograph on it, pinned to a notice board behind me.

It was only then that I realized my makeshift nose was dangling uselessly around my neck. The elastic had got overstretched in the crowd and lost all its spring.

'That's you!'
squeaked the
man. 'You're a
Wanted Outcast.'
He pulled a whistle on
a string from his top
pocket and put it in his
mouth.

*Right, it's now or
never,* I thought, and
grabbing the string,
I yanked the whistle
from the guard's mouth.

Thhhhp! He blew a raspberry into thin air.

Barging the flustered guard out of the way,
I hared down the platform as fast as I could in
my hot and heavy padding. The train was slowly
easing its way along the platform.

'Stop!' cried the guard.

'Stop!' I heard another voice yell, as I came
level with the door in the last carriage. 'Stop!'

I peered over my shoulder to see the cretin
Craik running onto the platform in hot pursuit.
Right behind him came the Guardian on his
unimoped, and the two raced along the platform
after me. *Oh, yikes!*

I shoved a metal luggage trolley out of my path and, as the train began picking up speed, I leaped onto a narrow step below the door and twisted the handle. The door swung open, with me clinging to the outside. It flapped wildly about, nearly knocking me off, but I managed to hang on and climb around to the other side. Then, as the train gave a sudden spurt of acceleration, the door slammed shut, and I was catapulted into the corridor of the carriage.

Leaving My Troubles Behind – Not!

I scrambled to my feet, ran to the door and peered out of the window. The tubby Guardian had driven his unimoped slap-bang into the luggage trolley, and was flailing about on the ground. Craik, though, was just outside the carriage door, running at full pelt and reaching for the handle!

Craik was reaching for the handle

No! I screamed inside my head. *Clear off, you creep!* Then, with a *whoosh!* everything went dark as the train disappeared into a tunnel.

When we emerged into bright sunlight at the other end, the train was zooming along, and there was no sign of Craik anywhere. *Phew!*

I nipped into the toilet and had a look at myself in the mirror. My dangling cardboard snout was dented and bent; one of my false eyebrows was stuck to my cheek and my hair was all over the place. I straightened myself out as best I could, tying the over-stretched elastic of the mask tightly round the back of my head, and reapplying my wandering eyebrow. I wondered if I should brave it and go and sit in one of the carriages with everyone else. I needed to keep a low profile though, so I decided it would be safer to stay where I was. I sat down and waited.

The train was rattling over the rails and going full pelt now, the scenery flashing past outside the frosted glass of the window. It would take at least four hours to reach Morph Wood where *somehow* I would have to find a way to get off the Bullet Express! I was feeling shattered and closed my eyes to rest them for a minute. But

I must have fallen into a deep sleep for the next thing I knew someone was banging on the door.

'Is there anyone in there?' asked a man's angry voice.

I woke up with a start, feeling confused and disorientated by the rumbling noise and flashing light.

'Could you hurry up, please,' the voice continued. 'There's a queue out here.'

Oh flip, I'm still in the train's loo, I thought, looking at my watch. *I've been in here for an hour! So much for keeping a low profile!* I unlocked the toilet door and stepped into the corridor. There was a queue of six people, staring angrily at me.

'About time too,' sniffed a ratty little man with a threadbare moustache and a comb-over hairdo.

'Sorry,' I said. 'I'm not feeling too well.'

'He does look a bit odd,' said another person in the queue. 'It looks like someone's given him a punch on the nose.'

'I'm not surprised,' said a round woman who was wearing a fancy fur-collared coat and had large front teeth as yellow as butter. 'Some people have no consideration.'

I pushed past them and hurried along the narrow corridor to where some automatic doors slid silently open. I walked through into the seating area, and looked for somewhere to sit. The carriage was full and everyone seemed to be staring at me suspiciously. I pulled the collar of my coat up around my ears and started to walk unsteadily along the swaying gangway.

I got another shock for, above the carriage windows, was a row of the Wanted! posters with my gormless face staring back at me. *Oh, heck,* I thought. *I really hope no one sees through my disguise, or I'm in deep trouble!*

I passed along the carriages until I found a place to sit, and slumped down in the seat. Looking out of the window, I saw that we'd left Fortune City behind us and its tall skyline was now out of sight. We were zooming along on a low viaduct, over the silvery sea that still flooded the surrounding landscape.

After an hour or so, the watery world petered out and we passed through an area of mudflats and rivulets that gradually gave way to rolling, low hills of bright green grass. It almost looked like a country scene from my own world, and I started to believe that maybe I was getting closer to home. I gave a deep sigh and, at long last, started to relax.

Then with a *swoosh,* the doors at the far end of the carriage swished open and I glanced up to see my worst enemy, Joseph Craik, enter. I couldn't believe it! Won't the great, gurning goon ever give up?

Craik keeps turning up, like a very bad penny!

Tickets Please!

Craik scanned the occupants with his one good eye. He hadn't spotted me yet, but it would only be a matter of seconds before he did. I pulled the collar higher around my face, trying not to look up.

Then the doors at the other end of the carriage swished open and I heard an officious voice call out, 'Tickets please. Have your tickets ready for inspection.'

Oh, jeepers, I thought. *I'm trapped on both sides.* I glanced around to see the ticket inspector slowly making his way along the carriage towards me. What was I going to do?

I wasn't the only one who was worried though. Craik's jaw dropped when he saw the inspector. His hand automatically went to feel for his money, but Snipe had emptied his pockets. Aha! If I was in trouble, so was Craik!

'Ticket please, sir,' said the inspector. I started and looked up. He was talking to me!

'Oh, I um, I didn't have time to . . .' I mumbled, trying to hide my cardboard snout behind the lapels of my coat.

'Are you all right, sir?' asked the inspector suspiciously.

'I've god a bad cowd,' I said, my voice sounding muffled behind my mask. 'I don't wand do gib you by germs!'

'Ticket then, please,' he said with a harder edge to his voice. People were looking at me now and, glancing over at Craik, I saw that he had spotted me. A horrible smile spread across his ugly mug.

'If you can't produce your ticket, sir, I'll have to ask you to accompany me,' said the inspector, taking a pair of handcuffs from his pocket and shaking them between his forefinger and thumb so they jangled. 'The Fortune City Express Company takes a very dim

Handcuffs!

view of fare-dodging and have provided a handy lockup in the freight car at the front of this train, for contingencies such as this.'

'You don't underdand,' I began, but the inspector was having none of it.

'OK. If you want to play it like that, put your hands out,' he said. Then I had a flash of inspiration.

'Oh, waid a minute, I'be just rebembered. I *do* have a ticked,' I cried, still trying to hide my face as I fumbled about in my rucksack, which I'd stored under the seat. My fingers closed on the mysterious ticket I'd been carrying about with me since the start of my adventures. I've no idea where I got it – I'm always picking up odd things that I think might come in useful one day. I handed him the scruffy ticket and he looked at it suspiciously.

'What's this?' he asked. 'A ticket to anywhere? I've not seen one of these before.'

COMPLIMENTARY

TICKET TO ANYWHERE
ONE WAY OR ANOTHER

DATE:
ANYTIME

16 2973

'Dere's nudding wrong wid it,' I said, staring at the floor so he couldn't get a good look at me. 'It's nod been punched, and dere's no date it has to be used by.'

'A ticket to anywhere, any place, any time,' murmured the inspector, looking confused. 'But, I've never heard of that.' He got a book out from the little satchel he had around his neck and started flicking through it. Then, to my amazement, he said, 'Oh, you're right. Here it is! The special *Ticket To Anywhere* ticket. I do beg your pardon, sir. Enjoy the rest of your journey, and I hope your cold gets better soon.' And he took his ticket punch and punched a hole in it.

I let out a sigh of relief and, as he carried on past me, I got up and headed in the opposite direction before he could change his mind. Craik got out of his seat to follow me.

'Just a moment, sir,' the inspector said. 'May I see your ticket before you go?'

'It's *him* you want,' said Craik pointing at me as I hurried along the carriage. 'He's the Outcast on those posters! Don't tell me you were taken in by his pathetic disguise?'

'One thing at a time, if you don't mind, sir. Your ticket, please,' said the officious inspector.

'I haven't got one. What are you going to do about it?' replied Craik with a sneer.

'Then I'll have to ask you to accompany me, please,' said the inspector, taking out his handcuffs again. 'If you wouldn't mind putting these on.'

'I'll put 'em around your neck,' roared Craik. 'Now get out of my way, you rat-faced twit.' He went to push past the inspector, but the little man was stronger than he looked. He grabbed Craik around the waist and the two of them wrestled and pushed and tugged and pulled. Then Craik tripped up the inspector, stepped over him and came running after me!

A Knockout Blow ☆

I ran hell for leather through the train, the passengers staring at me in surprise. I ripped the mask from my face and let the heavy coat and padding drop to the floor.

'It's the Wanted Outcast!' cried a woman in one of the carriages, pointing at the row of posters above her head.

Oh, flip! I thought.

'Stop him!' yelled Craik, already at the other end of the coach.

Two portly men jumped up at the same time to give chase, but in their haste they got wedged in the aisle, blocking Craik behind them.

'Get out of my way, you blithering boneheads!' bellowed Craik, grabbing one of the chubby chaps by the collar. I burst through the sliding doors into the next coach, and belted through it and out the other end before the startled travellers had time to register who or what I was.

I found myself in the freight car where large boxes and parcels were stacked in neat piles with narrow walkways between them. I could already hear Craik's angry yells coming from the carriage behind, and knew I had to do something quickly or he would catch up with me and I'd have no choice but to hand over my map.

I hid behind a pile of luggage trunks and quickly studied the layout of the carriage. Beyond the trunks and parcels, in the far right-hand corner, was the lockup. Its door was standing slightly ajar and I scuttled over to examine its locking mechanism. The door would lock automatically when it was closed, and I had the beginnings of an idea.

I looked up and grinned. Hanging in a loop from the ceiling, a little in front of the lockup door, was a chain. It was an alarm, only to be used in times of emergency. *This is definitely an emergency,* I said to myself, as Craik burst into the freight car.

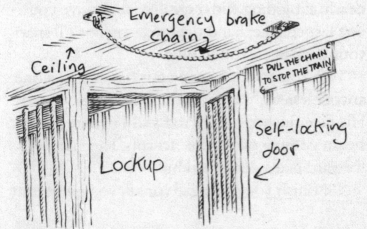

I could hear his heavy, rasping breath as he stopped just inside the door. I was still hidden behind the boxes, but I needed him to come towards me for my plan to work. So, taking a deep breath I said, 'You took your time, you wrinkled old wretch. You're getting too old for this game!'

'Grrr!' growled Craik and squeezed his way between the stacks of boxes until he faced me at the other end of the narrow walkway. I had my back to the lockup, its door now standing wide open. 'Think you're so clever, don't you, Charlie Small?' he said.

'A darn sight cleverer than you, that's for sure,' I replied.

'Well, *I'm* a darn sight stronger and more powerful than you, you little weed,' said Craik, nearly exploding with rage. 'Now, I'll give you one last chance; hand over that map or I'll snap your neck like a rotten twig.'

'Ha! You couldn't snap your fingers, let alone anyone's neck,' I taunted him. Well, that was it! His face flushed a deep red and I'm sure I saw steam coming out of his nostrils. He charged forward like a demented bull.

'I'll finish you once and for all, you interfering

little pest,' screamed Craik. He dived at me. I leaped up in the air, caught the chain above my head and swung my legs up out of his reach. The chain gave a

Craik nearly exploded with rage

lurch, activating the emergency brakes, and with a horrific squealing of metal the Bullet Express ground to a skidding halt, sending Craik pitching forward into the open lockup. He smacked his head against the wall on the far side of the cell and slithered to the ground. I jumped down and before my enemy could stagger to his feet, I slammed the door shut and locked him in.

'You swine!' screamed Craik, diving forward and trying to grab me through the bars. 'Let me out!'

'Yeah, right; like I'm going to do that,' I said. Then, hearing some of the passengers coming towards the freight car, I raced over to a large sliding door on the side, rolled it back and jumped down to the ground.

'You haven't seen the last of me!' yelled Craik as I hurried up the embankment. I squeezed through a prickly hedge, ran up a hill and across an open field. *Yeehah!* I had escaped!

Trapped!

Puffing and panting, I reached a thick, thorny hedge at the top of the hill. All of a sudden I heard shots ringing out, and looked anxiously back at the stationary train. Oops, I'd forgotten Craik had a pistol. A small angular figure leaped from the carriage and I knew my troubles were far from over.

I jumped into a deep ditch at the base of the hedge and ran along it, trying to keep out of sight. Spying a gap in the tangled, thorny branches above my head, I crawled out of the ditch and through the hedge.

The field on the other side was dotted with clumps of trees and sloped down to a cluster of dilapidated barns. Beyond those, on top of

a high, distant ridge was the dark smudge of a forest. My heart leaped with joy! *That must be Morph Wood,* I thought. *The portal back to my world is somewhere in there!*

I raced down the hill towards the ramshackle buildings. Halfway down, I heard a loud crack and *ptang!* a bullet whistled past my ear.

'I see yer, Charlie Small!' came a distant cry and, looking over my shoulder, I saw that Craik was already at the top of the slope. *Ptang!* Another shot rang out and then the fiend was running after me, his long, lanky legs eating up the ground between us.

Terrified, I ran for the shelter of a large barn. I dived inside and slammed the tall doors behind me. A thick wooden beam, hinged at one end to the doorframe, stood in an upright position. I pushed the beam with all my might and it swung down. With a mighty crash, the other end landed in a strong metal bracket and the doors were locked fast. I was just in time.

Crash! Craik barged the doors with his shoulder and the whole, rotting barn seemed to shake. *Bash!* He hit it again.

'I know you're in there, boy,' he called, his panting breath sounding hoarse. 'You're trapped, and I can wait out here for as long as it takes. You might as well give yerself up.'

I knew the despicable crook was right. I had to think of something, and fast. I turned round to see if there was another way out of the barn, and got the shock of my life!

The Steam-powered Elephant

Standing in the gloom, and filling the barn, was a magnificent metal elephant. I knew immediately that it was one of my pal Jakeman's wonderful inventions – a mechanimal, *here!*

I rushed over to it, taking in the rich detail of its shining, armoured skin. It was brilliantly made, with big hammered sheets of metal all riveted together with perfect precision. The legs were jointed and covered in chrome scales and dark grey chainmail. The trunk was divided into articulated sections, enabling it to move freely. There were long tusks curving from either side of its mouth and vicious-looking steel horns curving from its high, massive head. It was awesome.

'I'm still waiting,' called Craik in a singsong voice from outside. *Crack!* He fired a shot through the doors that sent splinters flying across the barn.

I darted around, desperately searching for the elephant's specification diagram that all of Jakeman's mechanimals come with. I eventually found it slotted between two of the elephant's steel toes and have stuck it into my journal for everyone to see. *Brilliant!* I thought as I quickly scanned the sheet. It works in exactly the same way as my old friend the Steam-powered Rhino!

Once started, the elephant was capable of refuelling itself by eating hay to burn in its internal furnace. The fire heated up a big tank of water, which the mechanimal refilled when it needed to simply by drinking. The heated water produced steam, which turned the flywheel, cogs and pistons to drive the machine forward.

(See my Journal 'Gorilla City')

Jakeman's Patented Steam-Powered
Battling, Bulldozer Elephant

Attack Horns

Saddle

Armour Plating

Armoured Skull

Steel Tusks

Iron Scales

Articulated Trunk

Steam Escape Valve

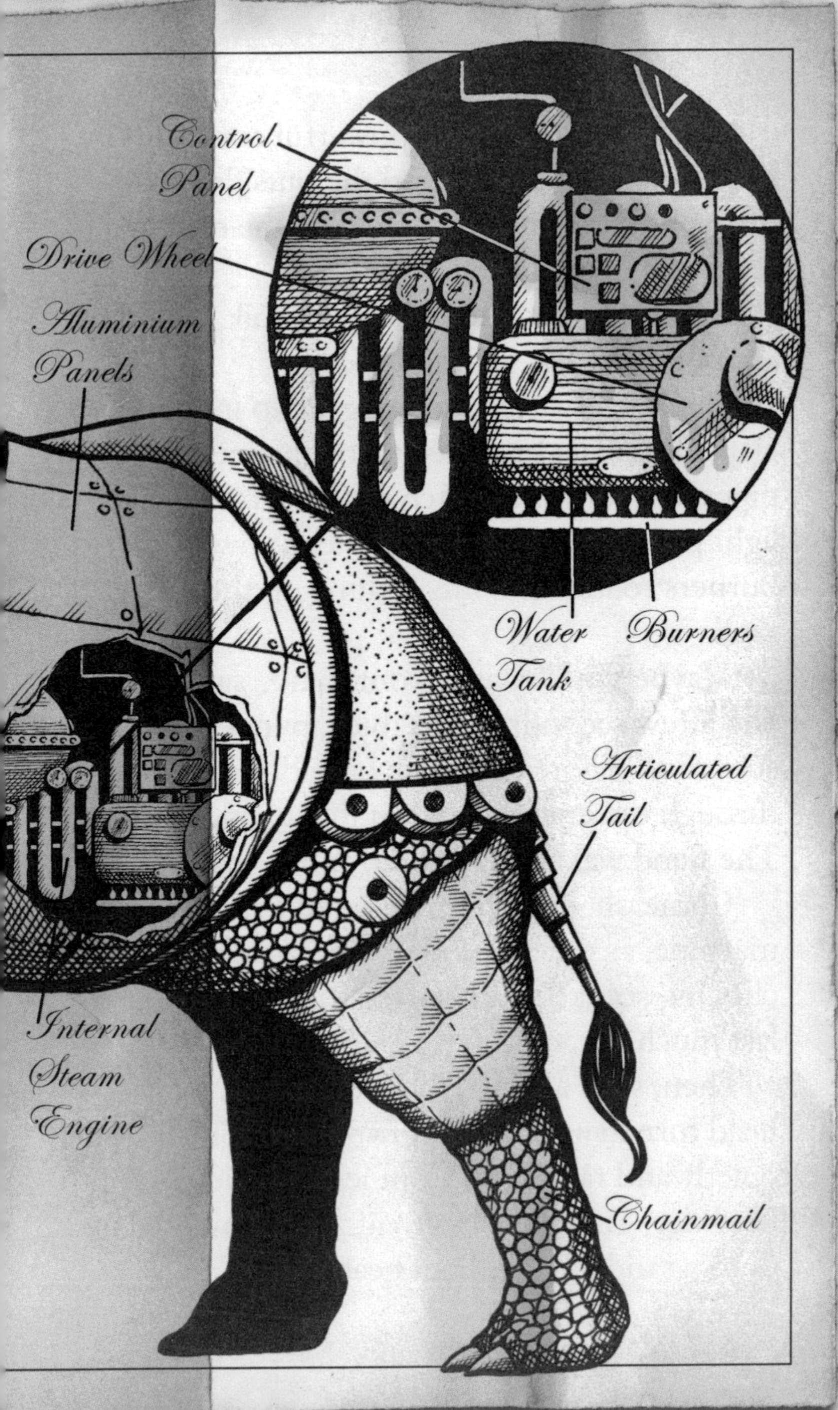

Control
Panel

Drive Wheel

Aluminium
Panels

Water
Tank

Burners

Articulated
Tail

Internal
Steam
Engine

Chainmail

It was sheer genius! A powerful computer in the elephant's head gauged the outside world through electronic eyes, allowing the machine to react and defend itself.

'Come on, Charlie,' bellowed Craik, sounding angrier now. 'I'm getting bored.'

'Get lost!' I yelled, opening a flap in the elephant's side. I reached through a maze of pipes and turned a switch to ON. A little pilot light popped, and a second later a row of burners roared into life, heating up the water tank.

'Maybe this'll change your mind,' said Craik, and a few seconds later a thick, pungent smoke started to billow under the barn doors and through the cracks between the wooden planks. The fiend was trying to smoke me out!

'Come on, hurry up,' I begged the motionless machine, as the barn filled with clouds of choking smoke and I started to cough. 'I can't last much longer.'

Then, with a whirr, the elephant's majestic head turned and stared down at me. She hissed quietly and raised her front leg and I leaped onto her knee, grabbed a large ear and clambered up onto a saddle behind her head.

'Let's go, Jumbo!' I cried and the huge mechanical animal stepped forward, steam hissing from the end of her trunk. Lowering her head, Jumbo pushed against the doors. The beam split, the gates flew open and we emerged into the sunlight.

Craik stared in disbelief, rooted to the spot as Jumbo crushed the bonfire with one of her huge feet, trumpeted and then charged. She scooped the stricken ruffian up with her tusks and sent him spinning through the air like a Catherine Wheel.

'Oof!' Craik gasped as he landed heavily on the ground, winded and motionless.

'Come on, Jumbo, full steam ahead!' I called.

The mechanical elephant carried on at a lumbering gallop, the ground shaking beneath her weight. As we headed for the hills and Morph Wood, I heard Craik yell after us.

'When I catch you up, I'll shoot you like a dog,' he bellowed and, *ptang, ptang, ptang!* Three bullets embedded themselves into Jumbo's metal flanks. Steam started to hiss from the holes, but the elephant kept on going.

Morph Wood

Over the fields we went, towards the forest that stretched across the distant skyline. We left Craik far behind, but I knew he would follow us. He'd never give up the chase now!

The further we went, the weaker Jumbo became. Steam whistled from the bullet holes; her metal joints began to squeal and I knew something must be seriously wrong. The elephant lumbered bravely on though, ploughing straight through any hedges that blocked our path.

It was late afternoon when we started up the final hill to the big wood. I had been travelling all day, but the excitement of getting so close to my goal made me forget my tiredness and fear. When we reached the top, I slipped off my rucksack and took out the compass and map. The dense wood stretched for miles and miles in both directions, and I needed to try and work out exactly where I was.

In the far distance to my right, I could just make out the faint line of the railway track. Behind me was the distant sparkle of the silvery sea, which surrounded Fortune City. To my left the line of the wood stretched away for a mile or so, before turning sharply left. I looked at my map.

OK, I thought. *That must put me about here*. I made a mark on the map with my pencil. I had travelled a bit too far west, but I wasn't very far off course. I checked my compass to see which way I had to go and gave Jumbo a knock on her metal cranium. It rang like a bell.

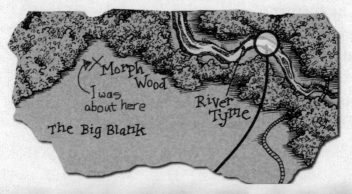

'Forward, Jumbo, forward,' I said. The massive mechanimal lumbered into action, squeaking like an old tin toy and emitting great sighs of steam from under her metal plates. We reached the edge of Morph Wood. The trees grew thick and the undergrowth between them was an impenetrable tangle.

'Forward!' I repeated, my heart starting to beat quickly with nerves. I was nearly home, but I knew Craik wasn't far behind. The elephant crashed into the wood, crushing thorny bushes underfoot and shouldering small trees out of her way. Apart from the noise we were making, the wood was very quiet. A hazy light filtered through the canopy of leaves overhead and gave the place a dream-like quality.

The River Tyme

The further we went, the denser the foliage grew, until we were forced to stop by a row of large trees blocking our path.

'It's no good, Jumbo,' I said. 'I'll have to go on alone. You'll never barge through this lot.' Jumbo shook her head impatiently and

trumpeted, as if to say *no way, just you watch!*
She pressed her armoured forehead against the
trunk of one of the trees and, using every last
ounce of her strength, began to push. Jumbo's
pistons hissed with the strain and the tree
creaked and groaned in protest. The elephant
pushed again and again. Then, as the tree started
to slowly topple over, there came a terrible
boom! Rivets shot from Jumbo's armoured flanks
and, with a terrific *whoosh*, a cloud of steam
billowed from a large rip in her side. With a sigh,
the elephant's head dropped and she stopped
moving.

'Forward, Jumbo!' I cried, kicking my heels
into the side of her metal neck.
'Come on, girl, don't give up
now.' But the great machine's
boiler had burst and Jumbo
was broken beyond repair.

I slid down from
the saddle and patted
her metallic trunk. The

*Whoosh!
A rivet shot from a
rip in Jumbo's side*

mechanimal's glass eye swivelled around in its
socket and looked at me.

'Thanks for everything, Jumbo,' I said as
the sound of hissing steam died away. A faint

light glowed briefly behind her eye, and then faded. I stood there in the silence for a minute, feeling sad and alone. Then I became aware of the sound of running water, and my heart leaped. *That must be the river!* I thought. *The River Tyme, where I will find the bridge to my world.* Brave Jumbo had brought me so close!

I hugged her cold trunk and then, feeling excited and nervous, hopped over the felled tree and pushed my way into the thick undergrowth. Thorns ripped at my clothes and scratched my face and hands, but I was too excited to let them bother me; I barged my way through until suddenly I was catapulted out of the bushes onto the grassy bank of a wide river.

On the opposite bank, Morph Wood continued, just as thick. The river's rich brown water seemed to chuckle as it flowed swiftly over the rocky river-bed, and a series of narrow, grassy islands stood in its middle. I glanced at my map and set off along the bank at a trot, searching for the portal back to my world. There was only one problem; I had no idea what a portal looked like!

I carried on, searching for anything that might be a doorway between two parallel worlds.

Was it just a tear in the air; an almost invisible, jagged crack that I had to step through? Was it an actual doorway I had to find – a door in a riverside boathouse, say, that would lead me down a dark passage to emerge in my own back garden? I had no idea, but I couldn't see anything that would do. There was only the endless, impenetrable wood on both banks and the gushing river between.

Then, as I turned a bend in the river, I saw an old brick bridge spanning the water a couple of hundred metres away. *That's got to be it!* I thought. Jakeman had said something about a bridge between two worlds. Maybe it was an *actual* bridge! It had to be worth a try.

The bridge!

I hurried forward, but almost immediately came to a juddering stop when I heard a crashing and snapping of branches. Up ahead, the undergrowth started to shake wildly, and then the formidable Craik limped from the bushes clutching his side and looking meaner than ever.

'Say your prayers, you irritating little scab!' he gasped, but he must have taken a right old battering from Jumbo because he found it difficult to raise his pistol.

The Final Showdown

I turned and ran round the bend and out of Craik's line of sight. This was my last chance of getting home. I had to think of something *fast*. I glanced up at the branches that arched overhead and a glimmer of an idea flickered across my panicking brain – but would I have time?

I let my rucksack drop to the ground and quickly took out the length of vine I used as a lasso. I whirled it around my head and let go. It flew up in the air and looped over a sturdy branch above me. I fed the rope out until the noose was nearly touching the ground. With the crunch of Craik's limping footsteps coming ever closer, I quickly shoved a few heavy rocks inside the rucksack and tightened the noose around it.

I heard Craik pause just around the corner as, with seconds to spare, I pulled down on the vine, and my rucksack, lassoed to the other end, rose up into the foliage above. Then, standing on the vine to hold it in place, I waited for my enemy to show himself.

Luckily, the foliage of the tree came down quite low and only a short length of lasso was visible above my head. Then it disappeared from view amongst the leaves, and snaked up to where my heavy rucksack was dangling.

'So, come to your senses at last, have you, Charlie?' sneered the villain as he

← Heavy rucksack

Vine loops over branches and is trapped underfoot

Me

Craik

staggered from the cover of the trees and saw me waiting with my hands in the air.

'I've had enough,' I said. 'I know when I'm beaten.'

Craik looked at me very suspiciously and snorted. 'That doesn't sound like you, Charlie Small,' he said, looking around as if he expected someone or something to come careering out of the wood. 'What are you up to?'

'Nothing,' I said. 'I'm just tired of running. I thought we could share the map and look for the portal into my world together.'

'What? After all this time you're willing to share your secret with me, when you know what I plan to do?' said Craik, even more warily. 'I wasn't born yesterday, Charlie Small. What's going on here?'

'Look,' I said, taking the map from my back pocket and waving it in the air. 'Do you want this or not?'

Unable to contain himself, the crook stepped forward, wincing with the pain from his bruised ribs. Now he was standing just below the hidden rucksack overhead. He held out his hand eagerly for the map, then hesitated and looked over his shoulder again, still expecting a trick.

'I don't trust you one inch, Charlie Small,'
growled the villain. 'So, I'm gonna keep my
promise and finish this right now.' He cocked
his pistol and aimed it straight at me.

'Just a mo!' I said with a gulp.

He stopped. 'What now, Charlie?' he growled,
as his trigger finger twitched greedily.

'I just wanted to say one last thing,' I said.

'Spit it out and let's get this over with!' he
screamed.

'Sleep tight!' I said, and stepped off the vine
trapped under my feet.

'Sleep tight?' repeated
the gormless goon. The
vine swished noisily
up through the leaves,
and Craik's startled
eyes followed it.
'What the . . . ?' But
that's all he had time
to say before the
plummeting rucksack
came hurtling down,
smacked him on the
bonce and he crumpled
to the ground.

Crunch!

I stared at him, making sure he was out cold before darting forward and retrieving my rucksack. As I fumbled to undo the lasso, he gave a roaring groan and grabbed me around the legs. I went down, kicking out and catching him a blow on the shoulder.

'You little blighter!' he moaned, his stubby fingers scrabbling for his pistol. I grabbed it first and threw it spinning into the thick undergrowth.

'Damn you, Charlie Small!' he uttered, as I kicked at him again and scrambled free of his grasping arms.

I got to my feet and ran, glancing over my shoulder as my dazed enemy tried to follow. He got up, staggered around as if he were drunk and fell back down in a motionless heap. At last, Craik was out for the count.

Tweet, tweet, tweet!

The Bridge

I ran as fast as I could, emptying the heavy rocks from my rucksack as I went. I pelted round the bend in the river and made for the bridge. As I clattered onto it, I glanced over my shoulder again, double-checking that Craik hadn't recovered and followed me. Then, looking at the rise of the bridge before me, I tried to spot some sort of fault or a ripple in the air, but everything looked completely normal.

Don't say this is just an ordinary bridge, I said to myself. I pelted across, reached the crest and kept on running. *Nothing happened!*

But as I ran down the slope towards the opposite bank, a loud rushing noise started to fill my ears like the crashing of mighty waves. The trees on the riverbank became blurred, and then a swirling grey cloud filled the world around me.

'*Whoa!*' I cried as my feet lifted from the ground and I felt as if I was spinning through the air. Images of people I'd met on my adventures appeared like flickering movies on the shifting cloud. There was Jakeman and Philly; the Puppet Master and Braemar; the Hawk, Thrak, Nemesis and Wild Bob Ffrance. All my friends and enemies floated before my eyes; Granny Green and Jenny; Captain Cut-throat, Bobo and Tristram Twitch; Belcher and Tree and Tom Baldwin and Mamuk. I called out to them, but my voice was lost in the rushing noise. Then the images flickered and were gone.

I began to feel seasick as my tummy flipped over and over and the rushing noise grew louder. I felt myself being stretched and stretched until I was so thin I could see straight through my own body, and was sure I was about to disintegrate into a million separate atoms. *'WHOOOAAAA!'*

CRACK! A bolt of lightning split the air and the churning cloud started to clear. The ground was rushing towards me at a thousand miles an hour. I closed my eyes and waited for the bone-shattering collision.

'Oof!' I cried, as I landed with no more of a bump than if I'd fallen over playing football. I felt as if I had been in a liquidizer though, and it took me a few minutes to get my breath back and clear my head. I looked around in amazement.

I had landed amongst clumps of wiry grass. Behind me was a river, but it looked narrower somehow and there was no sign of Morph Wood or the stone bridge. There were a few scrubby trees dotted about and a fallen tree trunk spanned the river where I had just crossed. I got unsteadily to my feet and looked around.

Then, suddenly I knew where I was. *'Yeehah!'* I crowed to the sky. I had landed on the patch of waste ground behind my house! The waste ground where I had set out on my adventures four hundred years ago. I had FINALLY made it home!

Home At Last!

Yeehah!

I ran along the bank of the swollen stream. I leaped over rivulets and jumped ditches until I came to the fence at the bottom of my garden. I burst through the gate, nearly knocking it from its hinges, and ran up the path to the back door and into the kitchen. Mum was dishing up the tea. I had just made it in time!

She looked round when I came in. 'Oh good, there you are, Charlie,' she said, as if nothing had happened. I felt a rush of relief and ran over and gave her a huge hug. Everything was just as I remembered it, four hundred years ago.

'It's so good to see you again, Mum,' I said, beaming like a loon.

'Yes, it must be all of three hours,' said

Mum, smiling and ruffling my hair. 'Did you get the milk?'

Oh, flip, I had forgotten the blooming milk! 'Sorry, I, um, I seem to have mislaid the money,' I said, patting my pockets. It was a white

Did you get the milk?' asked mum

lie, because I knew exactly where it was; on the counter of the sandwich shop in Fortune City!

'Oh, Charlie! I don't know; I ask you to do one simple thing,' said Mum with a long-suffering sigh.

'Decided to come home, have you?' said Dad with a grin as he came downstairs and into the kitchen. 'We were just about to send a search party out for you.'

'Dad!' I cried and rushed over and hugged him as well. He shot a quizzical look at Mum.

'Is everything all right, Charlie?' asked Dad.

'It is now!' I said.

'Oh, Charlie, just look at the state of your clothes,' cried Mum, noticing my mud-splattered trainers and ripped jeans. 'What on earth have you been up to?'

'Well, it started about four hundred years ago,'

I said, unable to contain my excitement a minute longer. I wanted them to know everything.

'I was sailing my raft down the stream when I was transported into another world and attacked by a monstrous crocodile. Then I ended up as king of the gorillas in a dark, dense jungle. No sooner had I escaped, when I was press-ganged by a horde of lady pirates.'

'Charlie,' interrupted Mum with a smile. 'You do talk a lot of nonsense. Go and wash your hands before tea.'

I slipped my ruined trainers off, kicked them into the corner by the back door and then went to go upstairs. At the door I turned round and looked at my mum and dad busy preparing the table. The radio was playing and a delicious smell of food filled the air.

'It's good to be home,' I said, and then leaped up the stairs to get ready for some of Mum's lovely grub.

Time For Bed

Well, I made it! I'm home, my adventures are all over and I'm just finishing writing up my journal. My tummy is bulging – Mum said I'd eaten enough for an army – and I'm lying in my own bed, surrounded by all my own stuff; my books and posters, my computer and games, my collections of animal bones and broken birds' eggs.

Now I'm home it's hard to believe all my adventures actually happened. I know they did though, because my rucksack is stuffed with the weird and wonderful things I collected on my travels. There are maps of exotic places, diagrams of marvellous mechanimals, plans of castles and secret passages.

There's a Barbarous Bat skull, a megashark's tooth and the bony finger from an animated skeleton! I've got a glass eye from a mechanical rhino, a tattered vine lasso, a cracked piece of shell-like coating that encased me when I was turned into a puppet, and lots, lots more. Looking at them now brings my adventures flooding back.

I wonder what all my friends are doing right now. Are Philly and Jakeman busy with a new invention? Is the Hawk galloping over windswept moorlands? Is Braemar the leader of his own pack of snowy-white wolves? I wonder if I'll ever see any of them again. Ah well, it was brilliant while it lasted – very scary, sometimes, and dangerous too, but great fun and I wouldn't have missed it for the world. It's time to get back to my normal life now. Back to exploring the waste ground behind my house and back to school. I can't complain – I've had a four-hundred-year holiday, and it will be really good to see my mates again.

This is Charlie Small, boy adventurer, signing off for the last time. Good night!

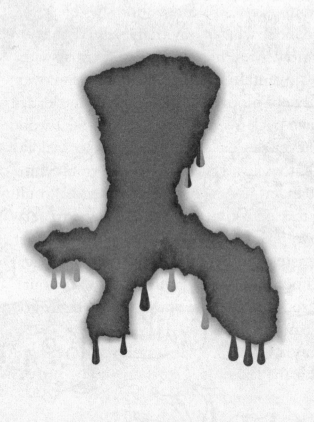

Two Years Later - Getting The Call

Well, I never! I've just found this old notebook hidden amongst a pile of discarded toys under my bed. I haven't seen it for *two years,* and I'd forgotten all about it. It's only because Mum is so fed up with the state of my room, and ordered me to bag-up some stuff for her car boot sale, that I found it at all.

I haven't thought about my adventures for ages, and flicking through this journal again I find it hard to believe they *actually* happened. They sound so fantastic, so implausible and it all seems such a long time ago. I mean, mechanical elephants, rat-faced felons and armed, piratical thief-takers? Surely, I must have imagined it. Yeah, I know I believed it at the time, but I *was* only eight.

Oh well, I'd better hurry up. The sooner I finish sorting through this stuff, the sooner I can go down the park and meet my friends, Niggle and Titch. There's bound to be a football match that we can join in with, and later on this afternoon my little cousin Alfie is coming over. Perhaps *he'd* like to have my adventurer's rucksack. He loves playing explorers and would be thrilled with my old journal, and the maps, bones, compasses and fangs!

But do I really want to give it all away? Just holding this tatty notebook in my hand makes me feel strange. Tiny pulses of excitement are flowing up my arm like little electric shocks, as if the book is somehow alive. Perhaps I should hang on to it, for old times' sake.

Whoa, hold on! Something's started chirruping inside the rucksack, like a demented cricket. I recognize that sound – it's my old explorer's mobile. After all this time, it's started ringing! But no one uses that number any more. My friends *always* call me on the mobile I got for my tenth birthday. Who the heck can it be?

'Hello! Who's there?' I asked. I don't know why, but my heart is crashing against my chest with excitement and I can hardly catch my breath.

'Charlie, is that you?' said a girl's voice, very faint and lost behind a swirl of interference. 'Charlie, it's Philly.'

'Philly?' Just a minute, where have I heard that name before? Oh, *jeepers,* I know! It's my old friend Philly Jakeman, the nutty inventor's granddaughter from the parallel world. Oh, wow! That means my journals are true. All those adventures really *did* happen. I *had* been a gorilla king and a pirate on the high seas. I *had* tackled a smoke demon that guarded a Mummy's tomb. *Yeehah!* I can hardly believe it.

'Yes, it's Philly. Oh Charlie, we're ___ trouble. I didn't _____ who else ___ call.'

'You're breaking up, Philly. You're breaking up!'

'Please ____ you come ____ save us. You do remember where ____ portal is, don't you? Hurry, Charlie, _____ we're being attacked by _____,'

'Philly?' I cried. *Darn it!* The line's gone dead. 'Philly, answer me.' It's no good. My mobile is out of battery.

Well, that's it; I've got no choice! I have to go back and help my friends. *Of course* I still know where the portal is; I used to go and stare at the fallen tree trunk all the time when I first got back, wondering if it still worked. Well, now I'm about to find out. Lucky I've got my explorer's kit handy!

I don't know what dangers lie before me, or how long I'll be away, but my friends need help and I *must* answer the call. There's just one problem. What am I going to tell Mum?

I know. I'll just tell her, I'll be back in time for tea!

The End

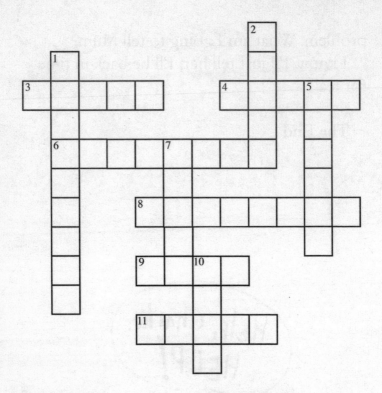

Clues Across

3. Mrs. - - - - - She looks after the Outcasts

4. I used it to haul my backpack up into the treetops

6. I keep my explorer's kit in here

8. The name of my hovering scooter

9. I met him in the mountains

11. My mechanical friend

Clues Down

1. They ride unimopeds

2. My arch-enemy

5. A Bush - - - - - -

7. He's my friend, and a pickpocket!

10. The name of the river in Morph Wood

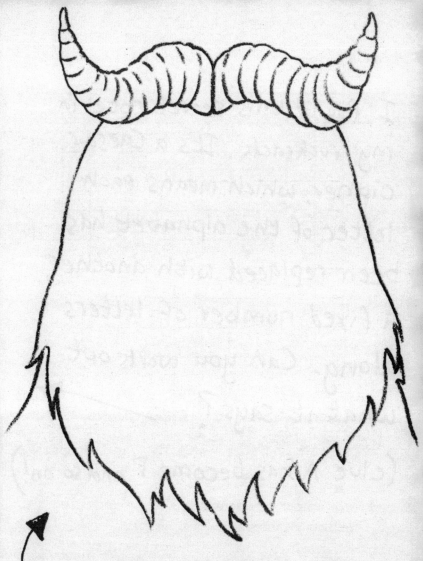

Draw your own yeti's face here.
Make it as scary as you can!

I found this secret note in my rucksack. It's a Caesar cipher, which means each letter of the alphabet has been replaced with another, a fixed number of letters along. Can you work out what it says?

(clue A has become P and so on!)

VDDS AJRZ,
RWPGAXT. X'AA
CTKTG UDGVTI
NDJ. X WDET
LT BTTI PVPXC.
ADKT,
    EWXAAN

X

A MARVELLOUS MECHANIMAL

INVENTED BY:

Design your own mechanical marvel here!

PATENT NO. 363612

Here are a few other monsters I saw on my travels, but didn't get time to write about

The Trilofighter has a serrated nose to saw up very hard prey, such as the leather-backed squid

The Cyclops of Cornucopia. He is very dim, but very strong, so WATCH OUT!

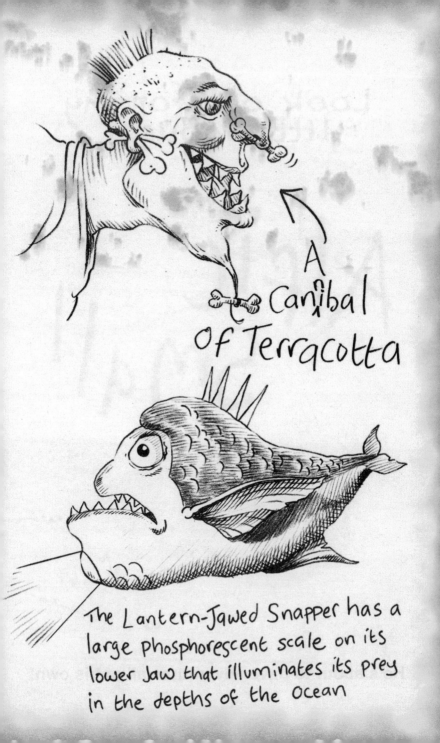

A Canibal Of Terracotta

The Lantern-Jawed Snapper has a large phosphorescent scale on its lower jaw that illuminates its prey in the depths of the Ocean

Look out for my little cousin

Alfie Small

He's about to have adventures all of his own!

I've found the portal
to the parallel world...

I'm crossing it!

I'm going...

I'm going...

I've gone!